## Project Gross-Out Begins

The other Bee Theres from her Beehive class were already at McDonald's when Carlie arrived. Keeping her voice low, she said, "I didn't explain too much on the phone, but this is why we're here. We're going to get rid of Rhoda. We need to draw up some plans."

All four of the other girls nodded.

"How about this for starters," Carlie said. "Since Sister Jackson thinks wholesome, let's think gross. We'll gross her out."

"We can sing off-key in the opening exercises," Elena said. "That would embarrass her, since she wants us all to be so perfect."

Becca nodded. "But that's not enough. How about if we pretend to be boy-crazy? In class we can talk about guys all the time."

"Yuck," Sunshine said.

Suddenly somebody said, "Well, good evening, girls. How nice to see you."

They looked up from their huddle. Standing there was none other than Sister Rhoda Jackson . . .

# GETTING RID OF RHODA

# GETTING RID OF RHODA

## LAEL LITTKE

Published by
Deseret Book Company
Salt Lake City, Utah

**Library of Congress Cataloging-in-Publication Data**

Littke, Lael.
    Getting rid of Rhoda / by Lael Littke.
        p.  cm.
    "Cinnamon Tree."
    Summary: Despite her reputation as "Most Wholesome" in her sixth grade class, Carlie leads her friends in a plan to get rid of the older woman who has replaced the well-liked leader of their Beehive church group.
    ISBN 0-87579-636-2
    [1. Behavior—Fiction.  2. Schools—Fiction.  3. Mormons—Fiction.
    4. Conduct of life—Fiction.]  I. Title.
PZ7.L719Ge  1992                                           92-25016
[Fic]—dc20                                                      CIP
                                                                 AC

Printed in the United States of America

10   9   8   7   6   5   4   3   2

*For Elizabeth Long, the original Most Wholesome*

# CHAPTER
## 1

Carlie was setting the table when the telephone rang. It had to be her friend Sunshine calling. Sunshine had told her at school that she would call before dinner with some secret news.

Plopping a stack of plates onto the table, Carlie yelled, "That's for me, Bart."

But even as she ran to answer it, Carlie knew that Bart was likely to get to the phone first. He was only four, but he was fast. His favorite thing was to answer the telephone, then chatter away as if the call were for him, which it never was.

There was no telling what he might say.

This time, as usual, Bart was faster than Carlie. He grabbed the telephone just before she reached for it, and said, "Hi. Who's this?"

Carlie tried to yank the handpiece away, but Bart had a firm hold on it. "Did you know my dog threw

1

up in my Mom's purse?" he said. "She had to burn it."

Carlie yanked again, and this time Bart's grip loosened. "She took the money out first," he yelled into the mouthpiece. Then, as businesslike as if he were Carlie's own personal secretary, he said, "It's for you, Carlie. It's your Beehive teacher."

Oh, no. He'd been telling all that grody stuff to Pamela. Carlie held the mouthpiece against her stomach. "Scat," she hissed at Bart. He scatted.

Carlie cleared her throat, then put the phone to her ear. "Hello, Pamela," she said, wishing she could make her voice sound low and smooth like Pamela's.

Pamela was laughing. "How old did you say your little brother is?"

"Four," Carlie said. "Isn't he gross?"

Pamela chuckled again. "Yes, he is."

She wasn't like other grown-ups, which was why Carlie liked her so much. Carlie's mom would have said something like, "Carlie Kuramoto, how can you be so hard on a little boy? You know he's just lonely."

But Pamela knew how things were, and that's why Carlie and the other first-year Beehive girls loved her so much. She even let them call her Pamela instead of Sister Sterling.

"Carlie," Pamela went on, "I'm just calling to tell everybody to be sure to come to activity night because

I have something to tell you. Some good news and . . . " She paused for the length of a breath. "And some bad news. And then some more good news."

Everybody was full of news these days. "I'll be there," Carlie said.

"And we won't be going miniature golfing the way we'd planned," Pamela added, "so you don't need to bring money."

"What are we going to do?"

"That's part of the news. See you at the church at seven-thirty. 'Bye."

Carlie hung up, picturing Pamela's face just as clearly as if they'd had phonovision. Pamela could have been a model or a movie star, but what she did was almost as glamorous. She was a flight attendant for an airline. She had hazel eyes and blonde hair that was cut short and blunt, making her look perky and cute. She had a figure that caused Carlie to gaze at her own skinny frame with despair.

"Carlie," her mom called from the kitchen. "Will you finish setting the table so we can eat? Dad will be home any minute and he has a meeting tonight."

"Okay," Carlie said, but her mind was still on Pamela. As she passed the hallway mirror, she paused long enough to squint at herself and think about what she'd look like with short, blunt-cut blonde hair.

It was hard to imagine. Her own hair was long

and black and straight. Her mom might let her get it cut if she coaxed, but she might as well not even ask about dyeing it blonde.

That didn't matter though. Sisters didn't always have the same color hair. For a moment Carlie let herself think about her favorite fantasy, that Pamela was her sister. She'd had a sister once, a big sister, named Ellen. She had died two years ago when she was fifteen and Carlie was ten.

Pamela was everything Ellen had been. Beautiful, understanding, and helpful. A perfect big sister.

"Carlie!" Bart came from the kitchen, filled with importance and authority. "Mom said you should get in there and finish setting the table. Mom *said*."

Carlie sighed. Pamela was always sympathizing with her and the other girls about how tiresome it was to be bossed around all the time. Pamela understood how it was to be twelve and powerless.

"Get lost," Carlie muttered to Bart. Then she folded up her fantasy and tucked it away in her mind like a secret note before heading for the kitchen.


Sunshine didn't call. Not before dinner nor after dinner either. But surely she'd be coming to activity night, since Pamela must have called her too.

Then again, you couldn't always depend on Sun-

4

shine. Her mother let her make her own decisions. If she didn't want to come to Mutual, she didn't.

Well, if she didn't show up, then she'd just have to deliver her secret news the next day. It could probably wait anyway.

Marybeth, Elena, and Becca were waiting for Carlie under the palm tree behind the church when her mother dropped her off. The May night was warm and they were all dressed in light clothes. Marybeth wore her flowered cotton overalls with a green shirt that looked great with her brown hair and freckles. Elena and Becca both wore long walking shorts and pastel blouses.

"Did Pamela call you?" Becca yelled as soon as Carlie got within hearing distance.

"Yes. Do you have any idea what's up?" Carlie hurried closer as she spoke.

Becca shook her head. "Maybe she's got tickets for all of us to go to 'Wheel of Fortune' or 'Jeopardy' or something. She said she was going to do that as soon as she could."

"But then what's the *bad* news?" Marybeth asked. "She told me she had good news and bad news to tell us."

"Maybe she could just get five tickets," Becca suggested. "One of us will have to stay home."

5

"I have a suggestion," Elena said. "Let's—go—in—and—find—out."

She sang the last words as if she were a country western singer, which was what she wanted to be. She listened to country western music all the time on the Walkman she usually had attached to her head.

"Maybe we should wait for Sunshine," Carlie said, "so the whole class can go in together." She peered down the driveway through the twilight of the soft, Southern California night as if Sunshine just might appear if she looked hard enough.

Becca started forward. "You know Sunshine. She may not get here until the Fourth of July." Walking across the cement entryway, she opened the door and motioned for the others to go in.

Several Scouts who were waiting in the foyer stopped tossing a basketball back and forth long enough to look at the girls.

It was Dale Delancy who started the chanting. "Buzzy, buzzy Beehives," he said, "looking for their honey."

That inspired all of the Scouts to start chanting. "Buzzy, buzzy Beehives, looking for their honey! Buzzy, buzzy Beehives, looking for their honey!"

Arvy Dixon went to the double doors that led into the cultural hall and yelled, "Hey, Jason! There are some girls here looking for you!"

6

Jason was the ward hunk, but it was a well-known fact that his eyesight didn't register any girl under fifteen. So even if he had interrupted the basketball game to come to the foyer, Carlie knew the girls had nothing to worry about.

Becca put the slimy little Scouts in their place with a look. "Shut up or we'll tell the bishop that you're playing basketball in the foyer. You'll be grounded for a year."

The Scout holding the basketball put it guiltily behind his back.

Carlie didn't even look at the boys as she went upstairs with the other girls. They were as bad as Bart, always doing dumb things. Whenever the other girls groaned about not being able to date until they were sixteen, Carlie thought of those Scouts and wondered why anybody would want to date anybody like that.

The door to the Beehive classroom was open, and good smells came from it.

"Chocolate chip cookies," Marybeth whispered. "This *is* a big occasion."

But Carlie was getting an uneasy feeling. She remembered Pamela's theory that chocolate chip cookies were for comfort. What was she going to tell them that would make them need comforting?

Pamela was there in the room, looking all aglow in a soft, loose melon-colored shirt, which she wore over black pants. The shirt seemed to light up her face. Or was the light coming from within her?

She wasn't alone in the room. An elderly woman sat on a chair on the front row. Her grandmother maybe? No, Carlie had seen the woman at church. She didn't always know the names of the old people, but she had definitely seen this woman before. She remembered the starched bubble hairdo that looked as if it belonged back in the Sixties.

"Come in, girls." Pamela came toward them, reaching out, giving them little hugs, handing out individual compliments to make each one feel good.

That was one of the many things Carlie loved about her. She did all the things a big sister would do.

"I'm glad you could all come." Pamela peered down the hallway toward the stairs. "But where's Sunshine?"

They all shrugged, silent now, eyeing the older woman and the plates of chocolate chip cookies. Not one plate, but six.

Six plates of cookies? One plate for each person? Carlie counted. If Sunshine came, there'd be seven people.

But maybe the elderly woman didn't eat cookies. Probably on a diet or something. Carlie's Grandma Shizuko was always on a diet. No sugar. No junk food. No fun.

"Well," Pamela began. "I hate to start without Sunshine, but we've got a lot to do tonight." She paused to listen. "Here she is."

They heard running steps coming up the stairs, and Sunshine burst into the room the way she always did, hair flying and her gauzy, longish dress barely keeping up with her.

"Sorry I'm late." Sunshine slid onto the chair next to Carlie. "Wait till I tell you the secret news," she whispered. "You'll die."

Carlie waited to die.

Pamela looked at Sunshine and put a finger to her lips.

"Tell you later," Sunshine whispered.

"Take over, Becca," Pamela said.

Becca, as class president, motioned to Elena to give the opening prayer. When Elena finished, Becca stood up and asked if there was any business.

There wasn't any.

Becca sat down again.

Pamela stood up. "It's time now for my news." She smiled at all of them. "Girls, I'm going to be married."

Carlie squealed right along with the rest of the girls.

"Is it Jeff?" Marybeth asked.

They all knew Pamela had been going with somebody named Jeff, although they'd never met him.

"Yes." Pamela's face lit up a few more watts, and Carlie knew the glow was all from within, not from the dress. "Look at my ring."

She held out her left hand so they could all admire the pretty diamond she wore on the fourth finger.

"Ooooooh," Sunshine sighed. "I can't wait to get old enough to get a diamond and be married."

"Time enough for that," the elderly woman said. It was the first time she'd spoken. "Enjoy your youth."

Nobody paid much attention to her.

"That's the good news," Pamela said. "Now for the bad."

Everybody quieted down. Carlie felt her stomach twist a little.

Pamela's eyes were bright as she looked at each girl. "The thing is," she said, "I'm not going to be your Beehive teacher any longer. I'll be leaving Southern California for quite a while. I might be in a different ward when I come back."

There was total silence. Pamela leaving? Carlie felt as if she had suddenly lost a sister all over again. What would she do without Pamela in her life? Who else wore clothes the way Pamela did, and stayed right up-to-date with hair and makeup styles? Who else drove a sporty little red convertible and sometimes took twelve-year-old girls in it on trips to a mall? Who else *understood*?

10

"I'm going to be married in September," Pamela said, "and I'm going home to Idaho for the next five months to get ready." Her smile widened. "But guess what! Remember, I told you I had some more *good* news?"

What could be good after what she'd just told them?

Pamela reached out to the elderly woman and helped her stand up. "You girls are so lucky. Sister Rhoda Jackson is one of my very favorite people here in the ward, and she is going to be your new Beehive leader. You're going to love her."

Carlie didn't dare turn her head. If she looked at any of the other girls, she knew she was going to cry. The only thing she could think of was that she hoped the news Sunshine had for her was a whole lot better than the bombshells Pamela had just dropped.

# CHAPTER
## 2

Carlie didn't even look up as Sister Rhoda Jackson got to her feet. She could see that the other girls kept their heads bent too. Marybeth even had a hand over her eyes. She was probably crying. Carlie didn't blame her.

"Girls," Sister Jackson said in a firm voice. "Look at me, please."

So that's how she was going to be. The schoolteacher type. Somehow Carlie had expected that she'd be the sweet, syrupy kind who would stand up there and smile and talk to them as if they were four years old, like Bart.

"Thank you, that's better," Sister Jackson said as the girls all raised their eyes. "I realize I'm not as pleasant to look at as Pamela is."

"She's got *that* right," Becca muttered in Carlie's ear.

Carlie was thinking the same thing. For starters, Sister Jackson was at least three times as old as Pamela. Her stiff hair was tinted a kind of orangey color that gave her a rusted look. She wore a gray plaid suit with a coppery-colored blouse and a gold chain necklace. On her feet were gray shoes with high heels.

She looked at if she might be headed to a Relief Society luncheon rather than a Beehive class activity night. And although all of her clothes were nice, they looked somehow old-fashioned, like her hairdo.

"However," Sister Jackson went on, "you'll get used to me."

For the first time, she smiled. She had nice teeth. All her own, Carlie decided, since she could see the gleam of gold fillings.

Sister Jackson picked up one of the plates of chocolate chip cookies. "We're going to be doing a lot of nice, wholesome activities, starting tonight. I'm sure you all noticed the cookies. We're going to do a service project tonight."

Carlie glanced at Becca, whose lips formed the words "service project?" as if she'd just heard them for the first time in her life. For this they'd canceled their miniature golf night?

"Ordinarily we'd have had a cookie-baking night together," Sister Jackson went on, "but there wasn't time. So we're just going to deliver these that I made

13

to the following people who need a little cheering up. I've already checked to make sure they can eat cookies."

Briskly Sister Jackson turned to the chalkboard behind her and wrote five names. Three women and two men. "You'll each carry a plate of cookies and make a presentation. There'll be one plate left to divide among us when we finish. We'll all travel together in my mini-van and sing camp songs as we go."

"Didn't I tell you that you were going to love Sister Jackson?" Pamela spoke for the first time since laying the bad news on them. "Come on, let's go."

Numbly, the girls followed Pamela and Sister Rhoda Jackson downstairs and out to Sister Jackson's mini-van. It wasn't old-fashioned, like Sister Jackson. In fact, it looked brand new. It didn't seem to fit with Sister Jackson.

Silently, the girls got inside and seated themselves on the two back seats, with Pamela in front with Sister Jackson. They looked gloomily at one another.

Sister Jackson started the car. "Okay, what do you want to sing?"

Nobody said anything.

Pamela tried to get them to sing "There's a hole in the bottom of the sea," but aside from a couple of bleats from Sunshine, nobody joined in.

14

"We're first-year Beehives," Elena said. "We haven't been to girls' camp yet. We don't know the songs."

That wasn't the total truth, since the older girls had taught them a lot of songs at firesides since they'd been old enough to attend. But nobody wanted to sing. Each girl sat stiffly, holding onto a plate. The smell of the cookies filled the car, making Carlie's stomach growl.

Sunshine leaned over from the seat behind her, and Carlie expected her to comment on the growling. But instead she whispered, "Want the to-die-for news now?"

Carlie shrugged. It might be nice to hear something cheerful.

"Well." Sunshine's voice in her ear sounded a little breathless. "You know the end-of-the-year newspaper that the sixth grade puts out just before graduation? Where they list all the 'Mosts' and all that other stuff?"

Of course Carlie knew about it. All the kids wanted to get their names in the "Mosts" column, like Most Popular, Most Talented, Most Likely to Succeed. She also knew that Sunshine was one of the kids who'd been working on the paper.

She nodded, and Sunshine whispered, "Well, you're one of the 'Mosts.' "

Carlie almost dropped her plate of cookies. "Really? Which one?"

15

"I don't know. I just heard Gregory Okinaga say that you were the best choice for whatever it is." Sunshine stopped to munch something, and Carlie suspected that she'd reached under the plastic wrap on the plate she was holding and pulled out a cookie.

Without even thinking, Carlie did the same. Her mind was totally spaced out by the thought that Gregory Okinaga—*Gregory Okinaga!*—thought she was the best choice for one of the "Mosts." Not that she was interested in boys. But if she *had* been, Gregory Okinaga was the boy she'd be interested in. Gregory was as tall as most eighth grade guys, not like Dale and those other stubby, wimpy Scouts back at the church. Gregory was sure to be named Most Popular. Gregory was super cool.

He wasn't Mormon, which was a drawback. Carlie knew her parents wouldn't want her dating a guy who wasn't Mormon. But she couldn't date anyway until she was sixteen, almost four long years away. But hey, if he already admired her for something, maybe she could convert him before then!

Carlie opened up her Fantasy File, letting herself see Gregory come up to her, fresh from the waters of baptism, saying, "I owe it all to you, Carlie." Then he'd ask her to the next stake dance. "Carlie," he'd say. "Carlie . . ."

"Carlie." It was Sister Jackson's voice. "Why don't

16

you deliver your plate of cookies first since you're nearest the door?"

Carlie realized they were stopped in front of a small beige-colored stucco house. Everybody in the car was looking at her.

Pamela hopped down from the front seat to open the sliding side door of the van from the outside. "I'll walk in with you." she said.

Carlie looked at the house. She had no idea who lived there. Had Sister Jackson told her while she wasn't listening? "Aren't we all going in?" she asked.

"No," Sister Jackson said. "The people on our list have all been ill or have a disability or else have recently lost a husband or wife. They might not be ready to have a whole group come in."

Carlie stumbled up the path toward the front door. Why were they doing this? She didn't know how to talk to strangers.

"This is the kind of thing we should have been doing all along instead of going to the beach and stuff like that," Pamela was saying. "You'll learn so much from Sister Jackson."

Sure. Rhoda Jackson had probably never heard of miniature golf, or "Wheel of Fortune," or the beach. Carlie had the feeling the Beehive class had seen the last of just-for-fun things.

"Knock," Pamela prompted as Carlie stood silently on the porch.

Carlie knocked on the door. It had been painted red at one time, but the paint was faded now and most of it had peeled away.

"Who lives here?" Carlie whispered frantically. "What should I say?"

Before Pamela could answer, the door opened. A woman, as faded as the door, stood there. Her gray hair hung straight to her shoulders and she wore a shapeless dark blue dress.

She looked at the plate Carlie thrust at her.

"I don't want any," she said. "And tell your Girl Scout people not to send you here anymore. I don't have money for cookies." She started to shut the door.

"I'm not a Girl Scout," Carlie said in a voice not much louder than a whisper. "I'm a Beehive girl. From the church. And I'm not selling cookies. I'm giving them to you."

The woman opened the door again. "Oh." She looked at the plate. Carlie looked at it too, realizing with horror that instead of the dozen cookies it had originally held, there were now only eight. Had she eaten four cookies while she was thinking of Gregory?

"Oh," the woman repeated. "Yes. Rhoda Jackson called me." Peering suspiciously at the cookies, she asked, "Did you make these?"

18

"No," Carlie whispered. "Sister Jackson did."

Lifting the plastic wrap, the woman took a cookie and sniffed it. She took a nibble of it. She chewed and swallowed, then took the plate from Carlie. "Why did you bring them to me?"

Carlie's arms dropped to her sides as if they no longer had any strength. "I don't know," she whispered.

Pamela answered for her. "They're a gift."

The woman squinted at her. "Little old to be a Beehive, aren't you?"

Pamela laughed. "I've been the Beehive adviser, Sister Durfee," she said. "I'm leaving, but you'll be seeing more of Carlie and the other girls."

To Carlie's surprise, Pamela stepped forward and kissed Sister Durfee on the cheek. "Goodbye now. We love you."

"Goodbye," Carlie said quickly, turning to go, hoping she wasn't expected to kiss Sister Durfee too. She heard Pamela's footsteps following her.

"Next time bring oatmeal," Sister Durfee called. "I like oatmeal cookies best."

Pamela stopped to say something, but Carlie didn't even wait to hear what it was. She climbed back into the van, knowing the other girls had watched the whole scene. She wished she could disappear.

"It's okay, Carlie," Sister Jackson said. "Stella Dur-

19

fee is a little thorny, but she'll be nicer the next time we go there. You'll come to love her eventually."

No way, Carlie said to herself as Pamela closed the sliding side door and got back into the front seat. There was no way she was ever going back to Sister Durfee's place. And love her? Get real.

Later, after they'd returned to the church and shared the last plate of cookies, the girls wandered out to the palm tree behind the building and sat down on the grass to wait for their rides home.

"So how was the person you visited?" Becca said. "Mine was an old man who cried all over me when I gave him the cookies. Said his wife used to make the same kind when she was alive. I didn't know what to say to him."

"I had to go right inside the house," Marybeth said. "Sister Miller has to stay in bed. She has tubes going into her arm and nose and has a nurse there all the time. She scared me a little, but she liked the cookies."

Sunshine's and Elena's experiences hadn't been so bad, but all of the girls agreed that they didn't want any more service projects.

For a few minutes they just sat there and stared into the darkness. The moon was high and the air was heavy with the scent of night-blooming jasmine. From the church came the yells of the Scouts, who had now been turned loose in the cultural hall with a basketball.

"Pamela didn't make us do things like service projects," Becca said. "I wish she wasn't going to get married. I almost hate that Jeff guy for taking her away from us."

"What'll we do without her?" mourned Marybeth, lying back on the grass. "Our Beehive class is ruined."

"Well, at least there's us," Sunshine said. "We'll always be there for one another."

Sunshine was the one who always looked on the bright side. Carlie sometimes wondered if that kind of attitude came with the name her mother had given her. Sunshine.

Be there, she mused. Be there for one another.

"You know what?" she said. "Let's have a club all our own. I mean besides our Beehive class. We can call ourselves the Bee Theres. You know—the B-e-e Theres. We can help one another through this."

Marybeth sat up. "I like that."

Elena jumped to her feet, flung out her arms, and sang, "We'll always Bee There, when times are tough. We'll always Bee There, when things get rough."

"They're rough already," Becca interrupted. "How much rougher can they be than having Sister Rhoda Jackson for our Beehive teacher?"

21

Marybeth groaned. "What are we going to do about it?"

Carlie scarcely heard. She was thinking that there was at least one bright spot in her life. Gregory Okinaga thought she was the "Most" something.

She would find out what it was the next day.

# CHAPTER
## 3

The next day Sunshine was waiting for Carlie at the top of the stairs that led down the hill to Baldwin Elementary School.

"Hi," Sunshine said. "Are you nervous?"

Carlie pretended nonchalance. "About what?"

They both giggled.

"Are you sure you don't have any idea which 'Most' I am?" Carlie asked.

Sunshine made a big X on the left side of her chest. "Cross my heart. And the newspaper won't be out until the end of the day. Maybe Gregory Okinaga will give you a preview if you smile pretty at him."

"Forget it, Sunshine." Carlie could feel herself blush.

To change the subject, she said, "Let's talk about our major problem. How are we going to survive Sister Rhoda Jackson? Our Beehive class will be totally zip if we have to have her as our leader. All we'll ever do is service projects and 'nice wholesome activities.' " For the last three words she made her voice higher to imitate Sister Jackson.

Sunshine squinted as she gazed out across the broad San Gabriel valley that lay before them. "Well, I like your idea about forming a separate Bee There club." She shrugged. "But what else can we do? You're the brainy one. Got any ideas?"

Brainy. Carlie grabbed the word. Maybe she'd been picked as Most Brainy in the whole sixth grade. That would be great. Gregory was a big brain himself and must certainly admire brainy girls.

But why make herself crazy guessing about that right now? Sunshine was waiting for her to say something.

With a sigh, she said, "I don't know. Maybe we'll just have to stop going to Mutual altogether." She looked at her watch. "It's time for class."

"Right." Sunshine turned to go down the stairs, and Carlie followed. She noticed how Sunshine's faded denim skirt had fringes on the bottom that gracefully dusted the steps behind her.

Sunshine always dressed in unusual clothes. Actually, unusual wasn't quite the right word. Strange was more like it. Today's skirt was so worn you could almost see through the threads in some places. With

24

it she wore what looked like combat boots and a T-shirt that was probably once blue.

But the funny thing was, on Sunshine the ratty clothes always looked good. It was probably, Carlie decided, because Sunshine was inside them. She had long, straight blond hair and kind of golden-brown eyes, not to mention a peach-like skin. Then there were her long, graceful legs and the way she carried herself.

If the "Most" committee had any sense, Sunshine would be named Most Stylish. She could make anything look good.

Carlie hoped her own clothes looked all right. She'd chosen her new pale red jeans. With them she wore a white blouse with small, pale red dots all over it and kind of a frill down the front. Red was one of the colors she looked best in. She wanted to look good on this day when people would be looking at her.

When Gregory Okinaga would be looking at her!

Gregory wasn't in the same sixth grade classroom as she and Sunshine. She wouldn't have been able to think about math or state capitals or anything else if he'd been sitting there in the same room. It was enough to total out her concentration just to know he'd noticed her. To know he'd actually *said her name!*

But the thing was, *why* had he noticed her?

The day was six years long instead of six hours.

The minute hand on the black-rimmed wall clock seemed to park on each number and just sit there. And sit there and sit there.

Everybody was nervous. Billie Lou Glenn kept combing her hair until Mr. Becker had to bark at her to put her comb away. Chandra Reynolds hummed softly under her breath and drummed her fingers on her desk. She was sure to be named Most Gorgeous or something like that.

Even Dale Delancy was fidgeting. Carlie remembered how he'd singsonged "Buzzy, buzzy Beehives, looking for their honey" last night at the church. She was still mad at him. She wished he went to another school.

Dale, Sunshine, Becca, and Carlie were the only Mormon kids in the sixth grade at Baldwin Elementary. All the other Mormon kids went to other schools in the city. Wouldn't it be great if all of them at Baldwin got mentioned in the newspaper? Well, all but Dale, maybe. He was such a nerd.

Just before the last bell rang, somebody delivered a stack of folded newspapers. Mr. Becker appointed Dale to hand them out. "Leave them folded until the bell rings," he ordered.

But he might as well have dropped his voice in the ocean, because papers rattled all over the room as kids began searching for their own names.

Chandra Reynolds squealed.

Carlie looked quickly at the front page, which is where the "Most" column was. There, right at the top, was "Most Unforgettable: Chandra Reynolds."

Underneath that was "Most Brainy: Ronald Blumenthal."

And next was "Most Friendly: Dale Delancy."

Most friendly? Dale?

Carlie hardly paused to think about that. Her eyes slid down the page to "Most Flirty: Gail Bennett," and "Most Likely to Start World War III: Kurt Lewis."

And next—there it was! "Most Wholesome: Carlie Kuramoto."

Carlie was so excited to see her name that it took a few minutes for it to sink in. Most *Wholesome!*

That was a Sister Rhoda Jackson word.

She leaned across the aisle toward Sunshine.

"Sunshine," she said. "What does wholesome make you think of?"

Sunshine stared at the newspaper. "Avocado and alfalfa sprout sandwiches," she said. "Buttermilk. Yogurt."

Carlie nodded. It described service projects and cannery assignments and Relief Society luncheons. It was nothing that a twelve-year-old girl wanted anything to do with.

Most Wholesome. Aaaargh!

But there she sat in her wimpy little red-dotted blouse with the frill down the front, as if to prove that she deserved the title.

She heard Sunshine groan in sympathy.

Wholesome! Why had Gregory Okinaga and the other kids done this to her? It was bad enough when they called her Molly Mormon for going to church so much, but this was terminal! It set her apart in a goody-goody world where *nobody* would ever want to come looking for her.

Was it supposed to be a joke, like the World War III one?

"Congratulations, Carlie," someone said. "Looks like you made the list."

"Thanks." She didn't even look up to see who said it, or if they said it with a smile or a snicker. She sat there staring at her name.

Sunshine came over to put her arms around her shoulders, and Becca came running in from the other sixth grade classroom to stand sympathetically by her side.

"How could they do that to you?" Becca whispered in her ear, "But listen. Sunshine and I and the other Beehives will always Bee There when you need us."

They were, too. They helped Carlie sneak out without having to talk to any other kids. They walked all the way home with her, and when she asked them to come in and stay for a while, they followed her inside without a word.

Carlie's mother was watching TV while she worked on her computer, which was set up on the dining room table. Or maybe she worked on the computer while she watched TV. Carlie was never sure which had top priority. Her mom did some kind of bookkeeping job at home, but she didn't want to miss the afternoon programs even when she was working.

She smiled when the girls came in. "Congratulations, Carlie," she said. "I heard you made the sixth grade 'Most' list."

How had the news got around so fast? Had Oprah Winfrey been interrupted to broadcast it?

Bewildered, Carlie looked at Sunshine and Becca, then back to her mother. "How did you find out?"

Her mother smiled. "I was talking on the phone with Sister Delancy when Dale got home. He showed her the list. Isn't it nice that both of you were honored."

Some honor it was to be on the same list as Dale. Some honor to be named "Miss Wholesome of Southern California."

But how could she explain how she felt? Carlie could just imagine what her mother would say. She'd think it was wonderful. She still lived back in the Fifties and Sixties, along with Sister Rhoda Jackson, when "wholesome" was what every girl wanted to be known as.

For the thousandth time Carlie wished Ellen were still alive. What she needed right now was a big sister who would understand what it was like to be totally wiped out at age twelve.

"Let's go upstairs," Carlie said to Sunshine and Becca.

"Bart's been watching for you to come home," her mother said. "He's lonely."

So what else was new?

"Tiptoe," Carlie told the other girls, "so he won't know we're here."

Silently she led them up to the room she and Ellen had shared. She needed to look at some of Ellen's things, the ones she kept in her special treasure drawer. She needed to feel close to Ellen so she could figure out what to do.

"Ellen would never have been named Most Wholesome," she whispered.

"But she was a real nice girl," Becca whispered back.

Carlie closed the door to her room so they could speak aloud. "I know that, Becca. But she didn't have to wear it around her neck like an albatross."

She repeated the last words. "Like an albatross." She liked the way they sounded. There'd been a guy in a poem Mr. Becker had read to them who had to wear a dead albatross around his neck. A real neat poem, but very long.

Ellen would never have worn a red-dotted blouse with a frill. A *sweet* blouse. Aaargh!

While the other girls watched, Carlie opened her treasure drawer and pulled out a headband Ellen had always worn when she ran with the girls' track team. There was the sweater she'd loved so much. And the T-shirt with the big golden cat face on the front. Ellen had been "with it." Like Pamela.

"Maybe I should call Pamela," she said. Should she tell Sunshine and Becca how she often thought of Pamela as her substitute older sister? Would they laugh?

"She told me last night she'd be away on a flight for the rest of the week," Becca said, "and then she'll be going to Idaho."

"Carlie." It was Bart. He opened the door and came right in.

"Didn't you ever hear of knocking?" Carlie said. She was going to tell him to scat, but Sunshine ran over to him. Picking him up, she danced around the room.

"How's my favorite guy today?" she said. "Did you have a hard day at preschool?"

"Yes," Bart said. "The other kids call me 'Barf.'"

Sunshine set Bart on his feet. "And what do you do when they call you 'Barf'? Do you say, 'Yes, and isn't it a lovely day?' "

Bart giggled, but before he could tell Sunshine what he really did, the telephone rang.

"I'll get it!" Bart ran out into the hall where the upstairs extension was. "Hello!" he yelled into the mouthpiece. "Did you know Carlie got voted Most Wholesome? I think that's something like the Holy Ghost."

He listened as Carlie leaped after him and tried to yank the phone away.

"No," he said. "At school. She got voted."

Carlie managed to separate him from the phone. "Scram," she hissed. "Leave. Go. Vamoose. Scat!"

He left.

"Hello," she said into the telephone. "This is Carlie. To whom did you wish to speak?"

"Well, congratulations, Carlie," said the voice in her ear. "This is Sister Rhoda Jackson. I'm very proud of you for making the 'Most' list. And as the Most Wholesome! I think that's a real honor."

She *would!*

She just simply didn't understand. How could she? She was practically on another planet.

"Uh," Carlie managed to say. "Thanks."

"What I'm calling about," Sister Jackson went on,

"is Sister Durfee. You know, of course, that she doesn't see too well."

"No," Carlie said. "I'm sorry. I didn't know."

"I asked her if she'd like somebody to come read to her once or twice each week during the summer," Sister Jackson said. "She said yes. I thought immediately of you, Carlie, since she already knows you. She can be your own personal service project."

Sister Jackson didn't give Carlie a chance to say yes or no or maybe. "Let me know on Sunday which days you can go," she finished and hung up. It was as if she'd given an order and simply expected Carlie to carry it out.

Carlie banged the phone down. This was going to be one great summer, with Sister Rhoda Jackson bossing her around every minute, making her live up to her new "wholesome" reputation. She wished Dale Delancy were in their Beehive class so he could scare her off the way he used to get rid of their Sunday School teachers.

Well, so did they need Dale for that?

Carlie picked up the phone again and turned to Sunshine and Becca, who watched her curiously.

"I'm calling an emergency session of the Bee Theres," she said. "We're going to have a little service project of our own. We'll call it 'Getting Rid of Rhoda.' "

# CHAPTER
# 4

Carlie saw Becca's eyes widen with alarm.

"Get rid of Rhoda?" Becca said. "How do you mean?"

Carlie laughed. "I'm not talking murder, Becca. Just something that will show her that being Beehive leader isn't the right calling for her. You know. The way Dale Delancy used to do to our Sunday School teachers."

Becca looked relieved. Then she smiled. "Yes. I remember."

Sunshine laughed. "Remember Brother Furley?"

The girls giggled, remembering.

"We were mean to him, but that's the kind of thing I'm talking about." Carlie felt a little guilty about what she was proposing. Sister Rhoda Jackson was probably a nice enough person, in her own old-fashioned world. She probably had a whole flock of little grandkids who adored her.

But she was just in the wrong job, and wouldn't it be easier on her if she left before she lost a lot of self-esteem? Maybe she could get herself a nice calling in the Relief Society instead.

Becca still frowned and twisted a lock of her long, red hair around her finger. She always did that when she wasn't sure of something.

But Sunshine looked ready to go into action. "So what do you have in mind?"

"I don't know. That's why I want to call an emergency session of the Bee Theres. I need to call Mary Beth and Elena." Carlie began to punch numbers on the telephone.

Becca reached out to stop her. She shook her head. "I'm not sure I like this. Why don't we give Sister Jackson a chance?" She looked straight at Carlie. "This isn't like you, Carlie. You've always been so ... so ... "

"Wholesome," Carlie finished for her. "And Sister Jackson thinks it's super great. If we stay with her we'll all be so nicey-nicey we'll gag the whole stake."

Sunshine opened her mouth wide, extended her tongue, and pointed down her throat.

Becca looked as if she were reconsidering.

"Close your eyes and think about Pamela," Carlie said. "What do you think of?"

Becca closed her eyes. "Sleep-over parties at her

apartment. Swimming parties. Miniature golf parties. Mall parties." She smiled.

"Now think about Sister Jackson."

"Service projects." Becca's smile faded.

She was definitely wavering. Carlie knew that the mall parties, when Pamela took all five girls to the mall and showed them what colors and kinds of clothes looked best on each one, were Becca's favorite activities.

"Well . . . ?" Becca's voice went up at the end of the word as if she were ready to come over to Carlie's side.

Sunshine joined in. "Next year we'll be *thirteen*, Becca." She said it as if it were a hideous disease. "Think of going through *that* without someone like Pamela to talk to."

Finally Becca was convinced. "Go ahead. Call Marybeth and Elena. Tell them six o'clock at you-know-where. Tell them it's urgent."

You-know-where was McDonald's on Lake Avenue. Last fall when Pamela had first become their Beehive Leader, she had said it would be nice to have a favorite spot to meet when things got heavy. "A place where we can eat while we talk," she'd said. "Food is so comforting."

The girls had chosen McDonald's. They'd had many a discussion over Big Macs and fries. Like the

36

time Marybeth's parents were thinking about divorce. And the time Elena was so upset but couldn't even tell them the reason. They'd met at the Golden Arches and munched their way through all their baby-sitting money while Pamela urged them to talk about their feelings.

Actually, Carlie decided, that had been the real start of the Bee Theres. The pattern had been set up then. Pamela had showed them the way. All they'd had to do was name the group.

"Guess where we'd be going to eat if Sister Rhoda Jackson picked the place to meet," Carlie said.

Becca snorted. "Harold's Health Food Hideaway."

Once again Sunshine opened her mouth wide and pointed down her throat.


After everybody promised to come to the Bee There meeting, Sunshine and Becca left to do their homework and get the necessary permissions from their parents to have dinner at McDonald's. There was scarcely ever any problem about permission, since the area was well-lighted and safe, especially at six o'clock in the evening. All of the parents approved of the five girls being so important to one another.

But Bart almost blew the whole thing when Carlie

37

went to the dining room, where her mother was still working on her computer.

Carlie didn't even notice Bart had followed her until she asked, "My Beehive class is meeting at McDonald's tonight. Is it okay if I go?"

Behind her, Bart said, "They're going to get rid of Rhoda." He came over to lean his elbows on the table. "Who's Rhoda?"

Mom looked up from her computer. "What's this?" Her eyes went from Bart to Carlie.

Carlie realized with alarm that Bart had heard everything they'd said up there in her room. He must have been lurking outside the door after she'd asked him to leave.

Getting rid of Rhoda was something Mom would be guaranteed not to approve of. And if Carlie's dad heard about it . . . well, did the church excommunicate twelve-year-old girls?

"Bart," she said in a stern voice, "how long since you've washed your ears? You're not hearing so well." Grabbing his right ear, she pulled it out as if to look inside. She managed to give it a little pinch before letting it go. "Hey," she said before he could yell, "how about coming with us to McDonald's? I'll buy you a Happy Meal." She hoped she had enough money to fulfill her promise.

Bart's eyes got big. "Can I? Mom, can I go with Carlie?"

Rhoda was erased from his mind. It was a desperate measure, inviting him to go with them, but Carlie didn't see any other way to stop his mouth. There was a play yard at McDonald's where they could send him while they talked about Sister Jackson.

Mom looked curiously at Carlie, but all she said was, "That's nice of you to invite Bart to go with you."

Then, as Carlie took a firm grip on Bart's hand and turned to go, she said, "Carlie, about Rhoda."

Carlie was sure her heart stopped. If Mom questioned her about what Bart had said, she'd have to tell the truth. She couldn't outright lie.

"Please call her Sister Jackson," Mom said. "I know you call Pamela by her first name, but Sister Jackson is much older, and you should show her some respect."

"You're right, Mom." Absolutely. In fact, she'd tell the other girls to call her Sister Jackson every time they spoke to her. It would probably drive her crazy.

Becca, Sunshine, Elena, and Marybeth were already there when Carlie and Bart arrived at McDonald's. They'd chosen the corner booth where they'd always sat with Pamela.

Elena was singing, and people were looking at her.

Sometimes it was embarrassing to be with Elena. She was likely to break out singing at any moment, like the cowboys in one of those old movies that Pamela had rented when they'd slept over at her house.

Elena liked country-western songs, and they were always sad. Like the one she was singing now, about a girl watching her sweetheart get married to somebody else.

People listened as they brought their food from the order counter and sat down to eat. They clapped when Elena finished the song.

Bart clapped too. "Sing the one about the dead dog," he yelled.

Elena and Marybeth and Sunshine and Becca turned to look at him. Almost everybody in the big dining room turned to look at him.

Carlie groaned. How was she going to explain why she had to bring a pest like him along to such an important meeting?

But Sunshine reached a hand toward him and said, "Hey, guy. Glad you could come. Are you going to sit by me?"

"Sure." Bart smiled happily as he slid a chair close to Sunshine's and sat down.

"Bart," Carlie said, "you can go outside and play on the slide as soon as you eat." She rolled her eyes at the other girls to show that she had to bring him but that they wouldn't be afflicted with his presence for the whole meal. "Actually," she said, "I guess we'll all have to go out there, since anybody under twelve has to be supervised."

"We can sit under the Apple Pie Tree," Sunshine said. "I'd like to sit there and watch Bart have fun."

Bart glowed. "How are you going to get rid of Rhoda?" he asked in a too-loud voice.

Carlie moaned under her breath. Why had she ever thought Rhoda had been erased from Bart's mind? She knew well enough that his brain stored every bit of information he ever heard.

"Whatever are you talking about?" she said to him. "What do you want to eat, Bart?"

She wondered if they should all just leave. What with Elena's singing and Bart's announcement, they were attracting far too much attention from the surrounding diners. How were they going to talk about Sister Rhoda Jackson with all those eyes and ears aimed their way?

But the other girls didn't seem too worried. "Let's go order," Marybeth said. "I'm starved."

Carlie ordered a Happy Meal for Bart, which left her just enough money for a big Mac and a chocolate shake for herself.

Bart was delighted with the spotted-dog prize in

his Happy Meal box, but he got fidgety before he finished his burger. "I want to go out and play on the slide," he said.

He had ketchup on his shirt, Carlie noticed. You could trace the history of Bart's meals just by looking at his shirt.

Carlie merely looked at the other girls, and they took the hint to gather up their food and carry it out to the Apple Pie Tree. That was all right, because the other adults in the play yard were standing by the slide and the swing, watching their kids.

Keeping her voice low, Carlie said, "I didn't explain too much on the phone, but this is why we're here." She went on to tell Elena and Marybeth about the discussion she, Sunshine, and Becca had had in her room. "So," she said when she finished, "we're going to get rid of Rhoda. We need to draw up some plans."

All four of the other girls nodded.

"I don't have any really good ideas yet," Sunshine said.

Carlie kept an eye on Bart. He was playing on the little merry-go-round thing. It was safe to get down to details without worrying about him hearing.

"How about this for starters," Carlie said. "Since Sister Jackson thinks wholesome, let's think gross. We'll gross her out."

Marybeth looked interested, but she said, "How?"

"Sing off-key in the opening exercises," Elena said. To demonstrate, she sang a couple bars of "Shall the youth of Zion falter in defending truth and right?" She was so gratingly off-key that she made Carlie's ears hurt.

"It would embarrass her to have such a tone deaf class," Elena said, "since she wants us all to be so perfect."

Becca nodded. "But that's not enough. How about if we pretend to be boy crazy? In class we can talk about guys all the time."

"Yuck," Sunshine said.

But that still wasn't enough. Carlie looked through the window of the dining room and saw a group of older kids come in. The two guys had shaved all their hair off except where they'd left some to form letters on the sides of their heads. She couldn't read what the words said.

The two girls looked as if their hair had never met up with a comb.

All four wore huge hoop earrings and leather vests.

She was still watching them when suddenly somebody said, "Well, good evening, girls. How nice to see you."

They looked up from their huddle. Standing there

43

was none other than Sister Rhoda Jackson. This time she was dressed in a pale pink suit with a creamy blouse and pearls. Her high-heeled shoes were a slightly darker pink.

Carlie wondered if she slept in beautiful clothes with matching shoes, with maybe an iron helmet to protect that perfect bubble hairdo.

"I was in there at the order counter," Sister Jackson said, indicating the dining room, "when I saw you out here."

Before she could say any more, Bart came running to the Apple Pie Tree. "Carlie," he whined, "there are some kids over there from my preschool. They're calling me 'Barf' again."

He stopped when he saw Sister Jackson standing by the table. He looked up at her, and Carlie could almost hear the circuits making connections in his brain.

Before she could think of how to stop him, he squinted up at Sister Jackson. "Are you Rhoda?" he asked in a loud voice.

# CHAPTER
## 5

"Bart," Carlie said, "where are your manners?"

As she spoke, she sprang from her chair and moved quickly to stand behind Bart. In a motion almost like a caress, she slid her hands down either side of his face, clamping her fingers together under his chin and pressing her thumbs against his cheekbones. That way he couldn't open his mouth without breaking his jaws.

Turning an innocent face toward Sister Jackson, Carlie said, "This is my little brother Bart, Sister Jackson. And this is Sister Jackson, Bart." She turned his head around so he was looking back at the figure of the Hamburglar on top of the slide close by. "Why don't you march right back over there and tell those nasty kids your name is Bart, not Barf."

Sister Jackson touched Bart's shoulder and turned him to look at to her. "Bart," she said, "I'll bet you can't guess what the kids used to call me."

Bart reached up to unglue Carlie's hands from his face so he could say, "What?"

Sister Jackson leaned down close to him and whispered something in his ear.

Bart's eyes widened. "Really?"

Sister Jackson nodded solemnly.

Bart giggled.

"So Barf's not so bad now, is it?"

Bart grinned as he looked up at Sister Jackson. Motioning for her to lean over, he cupped a hand around his mouth and whispered something back to her.

"Yes," she said, nodding again. "We'll make it our secret. Yours and mine."

Bart's eyes almost glazed over with sudden love. "Nobody ever let me have a secret with them before," he whispered.

Sister Jackson held out a hand. "Would you like me to walk you back to the slide, or would you rather go alone?"

Bart put his hand in hers. "I'd like you to come with me. You can go down the slide first, if you want to."

Sister Jackson turned to walk with him, the high heels of her pink pumps clicking on the cement. The girls couldn't hear what her answer about the slide was. It wouldn't have surprised Carlie if she'd gone down the slide, fancy clothes and all.

"Well," Becca said. "That's what Mr. Becker calls the 'whew factor.' "

Mr. Becker said the "whew factor" was when something came so close to happening that all you could say was "Whew" when it didn't.

Carlie nodded, running the back of a hand across her forehead. "I sure thought he was going to spill everything to Sister Jackson. He still might," she added gloomily, watching Bart whiz down the yellow slide as Sister Jackson cheered him on.

"She's really kind of nice," Sunshine said.

All the girls nodded.

Carlie thought she'd handled the situation well too. "She'd make a great Primary teacher."

"Probably she's had lots of practice with little kids," Elena said. "How many of her own do you think she had?"

"Probably seven or eight," Marybeth said. "Maybe nine. And tons of grandkids."

Becca nodded. "Tons. Anybody that old would have a lot."

It occurred to Carlie that if Sister Jackson had such a great posterity, she'd have had some experience with teenagers. Her kids would have been teenagers at one time or another.

But she didn't want to bring that up. Even if Sister Jackson had as many kids as the old woman in the shoe, she still wouldn't do as a Beehive leader. She could never be the understanding big sister Carlie missed so much.

Before she could say anything further, she saw Sister Jackson wave to Bart and head back to their table.

Was now the time to start grossing her out? They could giggle and be noisy. Maybe put french fries in their ears the way Dale Delancy did once when Brother Furley, their ex-Sunday School teacher, had taken them all out for a treat. That had finished it for Brother Furley. He'd asked the bishop for a calling in the family history library. Dale reported that Brother Furley told the bishop it would be a great pleasure to work with dead people, after that Sunday School class.

But nobody said or did a thing as Sister Jackson returned to the table.

"Girls," she said, "I'm really glad I saw all of you here. It saves me a lot of phone calls." Sitting down on the chair Bart had vacated, she crossed her ankles neatly and leaned forward. "You know that the Couth Youth banquet is coming up. And you know what an honor it is to be named the Queen of Couth."

The girls nodded. Carlie knew the others were

looking forward to the banquet as much as she was. It was the last youth event before the summer, and probably the nicest of the whole year. It was usually held at the bishop's house. The youth leaders and the bishopric and their wives served a formal dinner to the kids, with judges at each table to observe their manners and dress and conversation. At the end of the evening the King and Queen of Couth were crowned and were given nice prizes.

But wouldn't being the Queen of Couth be almost as bad as being Most Wholesome? No, because that was at church and all the kids considered it an honor. It was a whole different ballgame than being called "wholesome" at school.

Sister Jackson was still talking. "And so," she said, "I want to invite all of you to my home next Tuesday evening for dinner. We'll begin practicing for the banquet. I want our class to break all previous Couth records."

Smiling in turn at each girl, she rose and tap-tapped back inside McDonald's dining room, turning her head to stare at the kids with the far-out clothes and hair. She went on to the order counter. The girls couldn't see what she got.

"Probably a McLean burger and a wholesome salad," Sunshine muttered.

"I'm not going to any dinner at her house," Elena said.

"Yes you are," Carlie told her. "Don't you see? There couldn't be a better time to start our gross-out project."

Becca looked skeptical. "By doing what?"

"We'll think of something," Carlie said.

Marybeth gazed out toward the parking lot. "I wonder what it was the kids called her when she was young."

"I can't even imagine," Elena said. "Unless it was Patti Perfect."

The next day Carlie couldn't decide what to wear to school. Taking each piece of clothing out of her closet, she examined it carefully. If it was frilly or pink or in any way wholesome-looking, she put it in a pile to pass on to Deseret Industries.

She ended up wearing black bicycle shorts with Ellen's long black T-shirt that had the golden cat's head on the front. The cat's mouth was open, and it was snarling.

Just as she would snarl if she came face to face with Gregory Okinaga. She hoped she *would* see him. "What's the big idea?" she would demand. "What are you trying to do to me with this 'wholesome' business?"

Then he would smile . . . and her heart would go into a total meltdown and she'd make a great big fool of herself, just because he spoke to her.

No, she hoped she wouldn't see him after all.

She didn't.

But she saw a lot of other kids who commented about the great "honor" of being on the "Most" list. Clive Duggins said, "Hey, Carlie, why aren't you up there on the pole with the flag and apple pie?"

Clive would never be named "Most" anything, unless it was Most Repulsive. He was as bad as Dale Delancy.

Dale, who was picked as Most Friendly.

He must have bribed the kids who did the selections.

If it hadn't been for Sunshine's sympathetic presence, Carlie wouldn't have made it through the day. Sunshine was there, someone for Carlie to talk to. Someone to groan with when Mr. Becker proudly read the names of all the kids in his class who had been mentioned in the sixth grade newspaper.

That day Sunshine was wearing a pair of jeans that were held together by large safety pins, which on Sunshine almost appeared to be ornaments. The jeans were the envy of every girl in the class.

It was while Carlie was looking at those jeans that the idea began to form. She could scarcely wait until they were on their way home after school to tell Sunshine.

"Guess what?" she said as soon as they were far enough from the school grounds to have some privacy. "I know how we can gross out Sister Jackson."

"Tell me!" Sunshine stopped right in the middle of the intersection they were crossing.

Carlie reached out to pull her to the curb. "Sunshine, I absolutely adore your jeans. But what would Sister Jackson think about them?"

"She'd be revolted. Majorly revolted." Sunshine's eyes lit up. "I'll wear them to that Couth rehearsal dinner she's having."

"We'll all wear something like that. Safety pins everywhere."

Sunshine almost dropped her book bag. "She'll short-circuit!"

Carlie thought of the way Sister Jackson had stared at those older kids at McDonald's the night before. The ones with the weird hair and the leather vests. She wondered just how much she could do to her own hair without her mother objecting. Where could she borrow some leather stuff?

"This calls for another Bee There planning session," she said.

But she didn't get a chance to call one that afternoon. As soon as she walked into her house, her mother said, "Carlie, Sister Stella Durfee called. She wants you to come over to her house immediately."

Before Carlie could object, her mother went on. "Grab a snack while I find Bart, and I'll drop you off at her house. She didn't say exactly what it is she wants you for, but I got the impression it was very important."

Probably had something to do with Sister Jackson's offering her to Sister Durfee as a reader, Carlie thought. But how could that be an emergency? Had some other reader got Sister Durfee to the exciting part of a novel and she just couldn't wait to see what happened next? Or maybe it was something really serious, like needing Carlie to read the instructions on some bottles of medication. Maybe Carlie would save her from making a terrible, life-threatening mistake.

Her mother was shutting down her computer. "I didn't know you had become friends with Stella Durfee. She's not an easy person to befriend."

"Sister Jackson took me there," Carlie said. "She's my service project."

Her mother looked pleased. "Rhoda Jackson will be such a good influence on you girls." She smiled at

Carlie. "I'm so proud of you, sweetie. You truly are an example of a wholesome young girl."

Well, that blew any possibility of asking if she could do weird things with her hair.

Carlie thought about it as she went upstairs to change into her stone-washed jeans and a comfortable shirt to wear to Sister Durfee's.

What she decided was that Project Gross-Out was going to have to be another deep, dark secret.

# CHAPTER
# 6

Sister Durfee was standing on her front porch beside her faded red door when Carlie arrived.

Carlie thanked her mother for the ride and got out of the car. "I don't know how long I'll be," she said.

Her mother nodded. "Take your time. Just call when you're ready to come home." She started to drive away.

Bart leaned out of the car window. "Carlie got voted Most Holy," he yelled to Sister Durfee, waving as they left.

He was beginning to lose his grip on the facts. It didn't matter. Sister Durfee probably hadn't heard anyway, what with the noise of the car engine. Maybe her ears weren't any better than her eyes.

She squinted at Carlie. "Took you long enough to get here."

Carlie climbed the porch stairs, swallowing what she really wanted to say. All she said was, "Sorry."

She noticed that Sister Durfee's face looked pained. Was she having some kind of an attack? Maybe Carlie would have to call 911 and an ambulance would scream down the street with paramedics. Maybe the TV people would come and take pictures and there'd be a story on the evening news about the twelve-year-old girl who saved the life of a lonely, elderly woman.

She touched Sister Durfee's arm. "Are you all right?" she asked, worried now.

Sister Durfee looked up and down the street. "It's Deuteronomy," she said. "I can't find him anywhere."

"Deuteronomy? You mean your Bible is missing?"

Sister Durfee looked at her as if she'd lost her mind. "Deuteronomy is my cat. He's named after the one in the show *Cats*."

So this big emergency was about a cat? Carlie looked quickly down the street to see if her mother's car was still in sight. It wasn't, of course. For a dumb cat Carlie was postponing a really crucial Bee There meeting. She considered walking home, but another glance at Sister Durfee's face convinced her she should stay.

"When did you last see Deuteronomy?" she asked.

Sister Durfee wrung her hands. "Last night. I wasn't too worried when he didn't show up this morning. Sometimes he likes to prowl all night. But he hasn't showed up today, not even to eat. My eyes are as useless as a pair of peach pits, and I can't walk the streets looking for him. I want you to find him."

Find him. Carlie Kuramoto, Cat Finder. She could add that to her list of unwanted titles.

"I'll try," Carlie said. "Where should I look?"

Sister Durfee gave an exasperated sigh. "If I knew where to look, I'd go there myself. You're just going to have to go up and down the streets and call him."

"Call him?"

"He knows his own name," Sister Durfee said. "If he hears you calling, he'll come." She turned and went inside the house, motioning for Carlie to follow. "I'll show you a picture so you'll know him when you see him."

She walked across her small living room and picked up a framed picture from the top of a large, upright piano. "Here. This is Deuteronomy."

Carlie looked at the picture of a friendly dog face. "Didn't you say Deuteronomy is a cat?"

Sister Durfee snatched the picture back, putting it very close to her eyes so she could see it.

"Of course he's a cat. This isn't him. Can't you figure that out by yourself?" Turning back to the piano, she took down another picture and handed it to Carlie.

A fat orange cat peered at Carlie from the photograph.

"And take this." Sister Durfee held out something toward Carlie, something that looked like a dead mouse dangling from a string. It was gray and furry, with ears and a long tail.

Carlie shrank backwards.

"Oh, for pity's sake," Sister Durfee said. "It's just Deuteronomy's catnip mouse. It's not going to bite you. Here, take it. I want you to drag it behind you while you walk up and down the streets and call him. It's his favorite toy."

Drag it behind her? Was this really a service project? Carlie took hold of the string and started outside, groaning silently.

For almost half an hour she went up and down the streets near Sister Durfee's place, pulling the catnip mouse and calling out to Deuteronomy.

Twice she saw people sitting on their porches. They stared at her curiously.

On the street in back of where she started, Carlie met a small boy about Bart's age. He came up to her and asked if she was looking for Mrs. Durfee's cat.

"Yes," Carlie said. "Have you seen him?"

The boy nodded solemnly.

"Where?" Carlie asked breathlessly. At last she was getting someplace.

"Over there." The boy pointed to a wooden fence, just right for a cat to perch atop of.

Carlie ran over to it, looking for clues. A bit of orange fur, perhaps. Or maybe a barfed-up hair ball.

There were no clues.

Carlie looked back at the boy. "How long ago did you see Deuteronomy here?"

The boy wrinkled his forehead. "It was on Christmas," he said. "I remember it was Christmas because I was playing with my new roller blades."

Christmas! More than five months ago. The kid was some help!

"Can I pull the mouse?" he asked.

"No," Carlie said. "I think your mother must be calling you."

The kid listened. Although nobody was calling, he turned and ran home.

Good riddance, Carlie thought. A second Bart.

She trudged down the street again, heading toward Sister Durfee's house. The catnip mouse made a little skidding sound on the sidewalk behind her as she dragged it. It was a bit bedraggled by now.

There was one alleyway she hadn't searched. If Deuteronomy wasn't there, she was going to have to admit failure.

"Deuteronomy," she called. "Deuteronomy." She jiggled the catnip mouse and leaned down to look beneath the bushes that lined the alley. "Deuteronomy," she called a little louder.

No cat.

Great.

Disgusted, Carlie swung the catnip mouse around her head by the string. "Genesis, Exodus, Leviticus, Numbers, *Deuteronomy!*" she chanted, whacking the catnip mouse against the sidewalk at the end of her chant. Then she swung it around her head again. "Genesis, Exodus, Leviticus, Numbers, *Deuteronomy!*" Whap!

When she turned to leave the alley, she saw someone on the sidewalk, sitting on a bicycle. The sun was in her eyes, and she couldn't tell at first who it was.

"Hi, Carlie," the person said.

A boy voice.

She shaded her eyes with one hand.

Gregory. Gregory Okinaga.

Gregory Okinaga was sitting there watching her swing a toy mouse on a string and bellow out the first five books of the Bible.

He looked puzzled.

"What are you doing?" he said.

What *was* she doing?

"Nothing," she said. It came out a squeak.

He looked at the catnip mouse that lay on the ground now at the end of its string. "What's that?"

Carlie's face burned hot enough to fry her eyes. "It's just Deuteronomy's mouse." She cleared her throat. "Do you have cats?" She gathered up the string until the mouse was in her hand, then shoved it all in the back pocket of her jeans.

Gregory looked puzzled, but he answered, "Two of them."

"Do they ever hide from you?" Carlie asked.

Gregory's face took on kind of a cautious look. "They hide in the closets," he said. Then, as if he was afraid she'd ask more odd questions, he said, "I live here. I mean here on this street. I guess I'd better go home."

After another puzzled glance at her, he rode off on his bike.

Carlie watched him go. Her heart whacked her ribs. He was so mega-cute that it made her weak.

She realized suddenly that she hadn't told him Deuteronomy was a cat. What must he think of her? She must have seemed like a world-class weird-out, with that mouse and all.

This whole thing was Sister Rhoda Jackson's fault. If she hadn't started the whole service-project thing, this never would have happened. It was going to be a pleasure to get rid of her.

Her legs trembling, Carlie started toward Sister Durfee's house.

Sister Durfee wasn't happy when Carlie reported she hadn't found Deuteronomy.

"Well, go back out and look some more," she said. "He's got to be somewhere."

No way was Carlie going to go out there again, hollering for Deuteronomy, embarrassing herself into a stupor. "Maybe he's in a closet," she offered.

"He wouldn't be in a closet," Sister Durfee said. "He likes to go outside."

"Mind if I look?" Carlie asked.

Sister Durfee shrugged, which Carlie took to be a go-ahead.

She started with the entry-hall closet, which held two badly worn coats and a pair of rain boots.

"Deuteronomy?" she called. "Deuteronomy?"

She was sure she heard a faint "Meow" coming from somewhere in the house.

"Deuteronomy? Sister Durfee, did you hear a meow?"

Sister Durfee cocked an ear. "Don't hear anything but the kitchen tap drip, drip, dripping. Know how to fix taps? Drives me wild. Plumber wants an arm and a leg to come take a look."

"Deuteronomy?" Carlie called again. "Kitty, kitty, kitty."

She followed the answering meow. It was coming

from the central hallway. From behind a door at the end of the hall.

Carlie turned on the hall light and hurried to open the door. It was a linen closet. The light reflected from three sets of eyes.

Three? Were Gregory's cats in there with Deuteronomy?

"Meow?" said the big orange cat, who stood beside a stack of three towels on the middle shelf. "Meow."

"Deuteronomy!" screamed Sister Durfee. She reached into the closet and pulled out the cat, who rumbled with purrs as she hugged him. "How did you get in there?"

Carlie was still looking at the other eyes, which were behind where Deuteronomy had been standing.

"I think there's something else in here," she said. "There are eyes."

Sister Durfee came to stand beside her. She squinted into the closet.

"Must be my marten fur," she said after a moment. "Don't know what else would be in there that's got eyes."

She reached into the closet and pulled out a long fur neckpiece, the kind that has a little animal head at each end.

Carlie shuddered as she looked at it. Grandma

Shizuko used to have one of those, before she joined the Save the Wildlife Society.

Sister Durfee held Deuteronomy clamped to her shoulder with one hand while she dangled the fur with the other.

"I don't go anywhere that I can wear this anymore," she said. "Used to look so elegant, all dressed up." She was silent for a moment, then she said, "You deserve a reward for finding my Deuteronomy. Here, you can have it. Wear it to your prom."

She draped the fur around Carlie's neck. Carlie's first impulse was to snatch it off.

But it was just too gross to pass up. Carlie knew that she would never wear such a hideous thing to a prom. But she also knew that she was going to find some way to use it in Project Gross-Out.

# CHAPTER
# 7

Carlie worried all night about what Gregory was thinking about her and that catnip mouse and the way he saw her swinging it around her head. Was he going to spread it all around school that Carlie Kuramoto was terminally wacko?

Well, wasn't that one way to get rid of the Most Wholesome title?

She dressed carefully on Friday morning, putting on the stone-washed jeans she'd worn the night before. With them she wore a white T-shirt and a patchwork vest. There wasn't a single frill or ruffle on anything.

Sunshine was waiting for her as usual at the top of the stairs that led down to the school. She looked excited.

"Carlie," she said, "I've got an idea about what to do to gross out Sister Rhoda Jackson. You'll just die!"

If she died as often as Sunshine said "You'll just die," she'd have to have as many lives as a cat.

Thinking about cats reminded her of Deuteronomy, and that made her remember Gregory Okinaga all over again, and the look on his face after he'd seen her swing that catnip mouse around her head and wham it on the sidewalk while she chanted. If he blabbed about it at school, she'd be trashed.

Glancing nervously around to see if Gregory was anywhere in sight, she turned back to Sunshine. "I've got an idea too. Let's call an emergency Bee There conference tonight to talk about our ideas."

The bell rang then and they had to hurry to class. Just before they got to the door of their room, Carlie caught a glimpse of Gregory Okinaga. He was leaning against the wall by the door of the next room. He watched her with the same puzzled look as the day before. There was no reason for him to be there since his room was at the other end of the corridor. He must have been waiting there purposely to get a look at her. Very likely he wanted to see if she was really as goofy as she had been the evening before.

When he saw her looking back at him, Gregory turned and went down the hall to his own classroom.

There weren't any wild rumors flying around at recess, so he must not have told anybody about her. At eleven o'clock there was an assembly in the multipurpose room for all three sixth grade classes. Nobody whispered behind their hands as they looked at her. Carlie was grateful that Gregory wasn't talking.

Mrs. Waldvogel, the principal, conducted the assembly. She talked on about how outstanding the sixth grade was this year, in scholarship and leadership and behavior. She probably used the same speech every year for every sixth grade graduation assembly, but even so, Carlie felt proud of *their* class.

After she finished pumping them up, Mrs. Waldvogel told them how she expected them to be on their very best behavior at the graduation, which was to be on the south playing field at noon less than two weeks from that day. Carlie was to give one of the speeches.

Mrs. Waldvogel then spoke about how she expected them all to excel in junior high as they had at Baldwin Elementary. Carlie's mind wandered a little at that point as she thought of junior high and how it would be a whole new beginning. One thing she was sure of was that there was no way she was going to be known as Miss Wholesome in junior high.

The next thing she knew, Mrs. Waldvogel was calling her name.

After she said it she paused, and Carlie realized she was waiting for her to get up and stand with some other kids on the low stage in front of the whole group.

Numbly she got up and went to stand next to Kurt Lewis, whose name had been called just before hers.

When Mrs. Waldvogel finished calling names, she said, "There'll be awards and honors given out at graduation, but each year I like to single out those who have been picked by their peers as having some outstanding quality, even if it is Most Likely to Start World War III."

Everybody looked at Kurt Lewis and laughed.

"You people who are standing up here," Mrs. Waldvogel went on, "are the personalities who have impressed the others in your class, just by being you. Will you please step forward when I call your name again."

She cleared her throat, then read, "Chandra Reynolds, take a bow."

Everybody clapped as Chandra stepped forward and shot her arms into the air and did a little dance step.

Mrs. Waldvogel smiled. "Truly the Most Unforgettable," she said, then went on down the list. "Gail Bennett?"

Gail turned sideways and winked at the audience over her shoulder as she stepped forward.

Everybody clapped again, and a few boys whoohooed.

"Gail, Most Flirty," Mrs. Reynolds announced. "Dale Delancy?"

As Dale stepped forward with a big "Howdy," Carlie began to worry about what she could possibly do to represent Most Wholesome. Should she put a forefinger to her cheek and curtsy, like Shirley Temple in the old movies?

"Kurt Lewis?" Mrs. Waldvogel said.

Kurt took a Rambo-like stance and pretended to shoot the whole audience.

Carlie was next. Even as Mrs. Waldvogel called her name, she was still wondering what she could do.

As she stepped forward, Kurt said, "Hey, Carlie, did you know there's a string hanging from your back pocket?"

Before she even realized what it was, Kurt had pulled the string from her pocket and was dangling the battered catnip mouse in front of the whole sixth grade. It looked totally real, with its dirty, soggy fur and long tail.

Why hadn't she remembered to take that thing out of her pocket last night? Why hadn't she remembered this morning when she put on the jeans that it was there?

Some of the girls in the audience screamed. Even Chandra Reynolds put her hands over her face.

Carlie reached for the mouse and opened her

mouth to demand that Kurt give it to her. But just in time she realized that chasing him around the multipurpose room, whining for him to give her the mouse, would destroy her forever, or at least all the way through junior high, which might as well be forever.

So instead she grinned and quickly grabbed the mouse before Kurt could react. She held it up and sang out "Ta Da!" just as Mrs. Waldvogel announced "Most Wholesome."

The whole room exploded with laughter. Everybody was laughing, even Mrs. Waldvogel.

Everybody, that is, except Gregory Okinaga, who watched her with even more puzzlement than before.

But at any rate she had just avoided trading her Most Wholesome title for Most Weird.


The Bee Theres met at McDonald's again that evening for dinner. Each one except Sunshine reported that their parents felt that this McDonald's thing seemed to be getting out of hand, and didn't the girls think they ought to eat at home once in a while? Sunshine said her mom was always happy to have her eat elsewhere so she wouldn't have to fix anything more than the alfalfa sprouts and sunflower seeds she lived on.

Over Big Macs, Sunshine told the other girls about the sixth grade assembly and the mouse.

"What an actress!" she said. "Carlie acted as if she'd set the whole thing up the way it happened. It was terrific. Even Mrs. Waldvogel thought it was."

"But," Carlie put in, "she came up afterward to make sure it wasn't a real mouse. She said she knew I wouldn't do anything *that* gross, but she was just checking." She took just a moment then to explain about Sister Durfee and why she had the mouse with her in the first place.

"Speaking of gross," Marybeth said, "has anybody had any brainstorms about Project Gross-Out?"

Sunshine raised her hand. "I have."

"Me too." Carlie swallowed a mouthful of hamburger, then said, "You go first, Sunshine."

"Well." Sunshine put down what was left of her Big Mac. "You know how Sister Jackson talked about 'ladylike behavior'? Why don't we start acting like the boys? You know, throwing basketballs around and stuff like that. And." She paused to take a slurp of her strawberry shake, using the "and" as a hint that she wasn't finished yet. "And let's do the kind of things the boys do. When I passed Kurt and Dale and some other guys this morning, they were having a burping contest."

71

Elena looked shocked. "You mean *we* should have a burping contest?"

Sunshine shrugged. "Wouldn't it be worth it if we could get rid of Sister Jackson?"

Carlie thought it would be. If Sister Jackson hadn't introduced her to Sister Durfee, she never would have had that miserable catnip mouse in her pocket and wouldn't have faced what could easily have become the most embarrassing moment of her entire life.

Everybody except Elena agreed that it would be worth it. She kept shaking her head.

"What's your idea, Carlie?" she asked, apparently hoping it wouldn't be quite so gross.

Carlie explained how she'd noticed the way Sister Jackson had eyed the strange clothes the four motorcycle people were wearing the day they'd seen her at McDonald's. "So," she said, "I propose that we all wear really far-out stuff to her fancy dinner on Tuesday night. The cruddier the better. You know how she's always dressed so perfectly—and so ladylike. We'll tell her what we're wearing is the latest fashion, and she'll realize she's just not with it any more."

The other girls smiled. From the look in their eyes, Carlie knew they were visualizing what they might wear.

"I like both ideas," Becca said. "Why don't we do this: we'll wear the strange stuff on Tuesday, and if that doesn't do the trick, we'll do some research on gross stuff the guys do. That will be our backup plan to do on Thursday night at the Couth Banquet if we have to."

Elena frowned. "I'm not going to get into any burping contest."

"Maybe we won't have to do that, if the Tuesday plan works," Becca said. "Sister Jackson might give up right then and there."

Carlie looked at Sunshine. "How do you feel about it?" She didn't want her friend to think she was steamrollering her idea.

Sunshine grinned. "Listen, my mom's got clothes that will send Sister Jackson right over the edge. Let's meet at my house to get dressed for the fancy Tuesday dinner. We may not have to resort to a single burp."

"Then I'm with you, all the way," Elena said, and everybody cheered.

Marybeth waved a french fry. "Here's to getting rid of Rhoda on the very first try."

Everybody ate a french fry to show agreement.

Carlie was relieved that they liked her idea, and also that they'd be dressing at Sunshine's house. She wasn't sure how she could explain to her mother if she left the house wearing crummy clothes and that fur thing Sister Durfee had given her.

She yanked the battered catnip mouse from her

pocket. "Let's vow on the carcass of this critter that we'll never reveal our plan to another living person." She put the mouse in the middle of the table on a heap of napkins.

They each ate another fry.

"To seal our vow, let's return the mouse to its rightful owner, who I never would have met if it hadn't been for Rhoda, and that would have been fine with me." Carlie said. "She lives just three blocks from here."

"Rhoda the Rodent," Becca said, then clapped a hand over her mouth.

The girls looked at one another in realization. Rhoda the Rodent. That's what the kids must have called Rhoda when she was a child. That must be the secret name she'd told Bart the day he was feeling bad about being called Barf.

For just a moment Carlie had a twinge of real sympathy for a little girl who must have hurt a lot when people called her Rodent.

But did that make it any better that Sister Rhoda was messing up other people's lives now?

"Come on," Carlie said, "let's get this mouse back to Deuteronomy. He must be missing it."

When they got outside they were super giggly, probably because they'd finally settled on a plan for Project Gross-Out. Or maybe they were trying to avoid thinking about the unhappy little girl Rhoda must have been at one time.

The other girls insisted that Carlie drag the catnip mouse behind her on the string again as they walked toward Sister Durfee's house. Feeling a little light-headed herself, she dragged it for a while, then swung it around her head the way she'd done the night before. "Genesis, Exodus, Leviticus, Numbers, Deuteronomy!" she chanted again.

The other girls joined in, giggling more than they chanted.

Carlie was so hyper that she didn't mind that people stared at them. Not until Gregory Okinaga came along on his bike, heading toward McDonald's.

Oh, no. Why hadn't she remembered that he lived right there in the neighborhood, close to Sister Durfee? Why hadn't she ditched that disgusting mouse somewhere in a trash can?

Gregory skidded his bike to a stop and outright stared. His eyes went from the mouse to Carlie, and his look of puzzlement was replaced by one of total bafflement.

# CHAPTER
# 8

Carlie's life was on a definite downhill slide. What was there to say to Gregory that would make things any better? How could she possibly explain?

She didn't get a chance to explain. After a tentative "Hi, Carlie," Gregory rode off.

Things didn't go much better at Sister Durfee's house when Carlie and the other girls got there. Sister Durfee didn't want the much-traveled catnip mouse when Carlie offered it to her.

She squinted at it, then shoved it back to Carlie. "Keep it. Deuteronomy hates dirty toys."

It was a mild reprimand, since the catnip mouse had been fairly clean when she gave it to Carlie.

On the other hand, *she* was the one who had said Carlie should drag it along the streets. It was *her* fault it was dirty. Actually, it was Sister Rhoda Jackson's fault, since she started all of this.

Once again Carlie had to bite back what she really wanted to say. Clearing her throat to get rid of the sharp words, she said, "I'm glad Deuteronomy is behaving himself and isn't hiding in any more closets." She gestured toward the big orange cat, which perched beside a bright geranium of almost the same color on the front windowsill. Beside him a prism scattered the light coming through it, making pretty colored spots throughout the room.

Sister Durfee had been looking at Sunshine and Elena and Marybeth and Becca. Now she returned her squint to Carlie. "Why would he hide in a closet?" She sounded offended.

Carlie didn't know what to say. She'd just been making conversation. She felt a little embarrassed there in front of the other girls.

She gave a small laugh to show that her intentions were good. "Well, since he did it once, I thought he might do it again."

From his perch on the windowsill, Deuteronomy stared insolently at her through slitted eyes, then sat down to wash his face.

"You never did tell me just exactly how you knew he was in the linen closet," Sister Durfee said, her eyes slitting like Deuteronomy's. It was almost an accusation.

It was clearly time to leave. Dropping the catnip

mouse into the small purse she carried, Carlie said, "It's been nice visiting with you, Sister Durfee. I guess we'd better go now."

"Aren't you going to read to me?" Sister Durfee asked. "I called your house and said I needed somebody to read."

Carlie started toward the door, motioning for the others to go ahead of her. "I haven't been home to get the message, and I can't stay right now, Sister Durfee. But I'll come back tomorrow and read to you. Is that okay?"

Sister Durfee made a hmmphing sound. "Fine kettle of fish," she muttered.

Carlie's face felt hot. "How about eleven o'clock tomorrow? It's Saturday and I don't have to go to school."

"If that's all you can manage," Sister Durfee sniffed. "Don't bring all these people with you." She flapped her hands at the other girls. "Crowds make me nervous. You should know that."

Sunshine, Elena, Marybeth, and Becca could scarcely hold their giggles until they were outside. Halfway down the street they stopped to laugh so hard they almost had to sit down.

Still giggling, Marybeth licked the tip of a forefinger and made a check mark in the air. "That's one point for Sister Rhoda Jackson," she said.

Carlie didn't understand. "What do you mean?"

Marybeth put an arm around Carlie's shoulders. "Sister Jackson gave that service project to you and not to me. So that's a point in her favor in my book."

Carlie felt she should have joined in the laughter with the others, but she didn't. It was true that Sister Durfee was a real pain. But the other girls hadn't seen her face the day before when she had thought her cat was lost.

Later, alone in her room, Carlie took the catnip mouse out of her purse and dropped it into a wastebasket. It had caused enough trouble.

This certainly hadn't been one of her best days. It made her worry again about Project Gross-Out. Sunshine's mom was always talking about horoscopes and planets being in alignment and all that kind of stuff. Maybe Carlie's planets were out of whack and nothing she attempted would go right. Maybe she should ask Sunshine's mom.

On the other hand, if dressing weird on Tuesday night failed, the Bee Theres could always fall back on Plan Number Two, which was to do the gross things the boys did.

Since she was alone in her bedroom, Carlie decided to try burping just in case they had to resort to that. Swallowing air, she tried to bring it back up with a lot of noise. It certainly looked easy enough when Dale and Kurt and the other guys did it.

She tried until her throat muscles hurt, but it was hopeless. Burping wasn't one of her talents. Another failure.

Maybe she could get Dale to tutor her. He would probably be more than pleased to teach her.

But surely they wouldn't have to go that far. No, Tuesday night was going to do it.

Thoughtfully she picked the catnip mouse out of the wastebasket and tucked it back inside her purse. You just never knew when something like that might come in handy.


Sister Rhoda Jackson was going to be officially sustained as Beehive leader at sacrament meeting on Sunday. On Saturday morning Carlie and the other Bee Theres made plans over the telephone. They agreed that when the bishop asked for all those in favor of sustaining her to show it by the uplifted hand, they would only semi-raise theirs. They were going to lift them far enough to fiddle with their hair, or adjust an earring, or scratch a nose. They wouldn't be sitting together, since their parents liked them to sit with their families during that meeting, so probably no one would notice that they didn't really sustain Sister Rhoda.

The rest of Saturday wasn't all that bad. Carlie spent most of the day at Sister Durfee's house, sitting in the comfortable green wing chair, reading to her from whatever was lying around the house—the *Ensign*, the *Reader's Digest*, a couple of romance novels she found on a bookshelf.

One of the romances wasn't bad. It was about Megan, who works in a sporting goods store. Tall, athletic Trevor comes in to buy some bungee cords to do some jumping with them. Megan, who has a date that night with Elwood, a tax accountant, is impressed with his daring. Trevor invites her to go along with him, but of course she refuses since she just met him. But all that evening with Elwood, she thinks of Trevor.

Carlie can't blame her. It was like comparing Dale Delancy with Gregory Okinaga.

Sister Durfee listened quietly to the reading, with Deuteronomy asleep on her lap. "Who do you think is going to win the girl?" she asked when Carlie finished the first chapter of the romance.

Without even thinking, Carlie said, "Trevor."

Sister Durfee smiled. "But Elwood is a nice, steady fellow. Trevor is apt to break his neck with that bungee-cord jumping."

"But Elwood's such a lump," Carlie objected.

81

"Look at the title," Sister Durfee said.

Carlie flipped the book closed and looked. The title was *All That Glitters*.

" 'All that glitters is not gold,' " she said. Everybody knew that quotation.

"Do you think that means Trevor might not be all that he appears to be?" Sister Durfee asked.

Carlie didn't like to think of that.

"Or," Sister Durfee said, "do you think it's going to be a switcheroo and Megan will find that what glitters just might *be* gold?"

Sister Durfee was pretty smart. Carlie hadn't thought of turning the quotation around that way.

"Maybe," she said.

"I guess we won't know until we read the book," Sister Durfee said. "You can go now, Carlie. I want to take a nap."

Carlie was glad to leave.

On Sunday she sat with her mother and Bart at church. Her father was giving a high council talk in another ward, so he wasn't there.

Carlie noticed right away that Sister Jackson was three rows in front of her. As always she was dressed to perfection, every hair glued in place and everything she wore totally coordinated. Her dress was pale blue with a blue plaid belt. Her earrings were pale blue with crisscross lines of the same colors as in the plaid, and her purse picked up the same colors too. Carlie couldn't see her shoes, but she knew without a doubt they would be dark blue. She wouldn't have been surprised if they'd been plaid.

Everything was, as usual, very nice but several years out of date.

All during the opening hymn and the prayer, Carlie thought about how Sister Jackson must select what to wear. Which item did she start out with? Did she pick a dress first, then start to match up everything? Or did she buy it all matched in the first place?

The bishop stood up and began the business part of the meeting.

"It has become necessary to release Brother Dave Arden as the Sunday School president," he announced. "We'll do that now with a vote of thanks for his fine service. All in favor please manifest it by the uplifted hand."

As far as Carlie could see, every right hand in the congregation went up, including Sister Jackson's. She was wearing a large dark-blue ring on the fourth finger of her right hand.

What would happen if Sister Jackson got dressed and didn't have the right color ring? Or worse, what if she couldn't find the matching purse? Would her whole personality break down if she wasn't coordinated?

The bishop proposed sustaining somebody as the new Sunday School president and again hands rose.

"Any opposed, please indicate by the same sign," he said.

No hands went up that time. The bishop proceeded on to some changes in the Relief Society. "All in favor?" Right hands rose and fell. "Any opposed?"

The air conditioner hissed softly. Carlie's mind wandered through Sister Jackson's closet. Did she have everything hung together, with rings and earrings and stuff in little plastic bags attached to hangers with the dresses? And maybe the shoes standing neatly underneath?

" . . . release Sister Pamela Spencer with a vote of thanks," Carlie heard the bishop say. "All in favor?" She raised her hand automatically.

Pamela! Oh, how she wished Pamela didn't have to be released. Pamela, her almost-sister, whose guidance she'd been counting on to get her through her early teen years.

Beside her, Bart raised his hand as high as he could with each vote of thanks or sustaining. Bart liked this active part of the meeting, but usually slept later on.

Carlie felt drowsy herself.

"Sister Rhoda Jackson . . . ," she heard the bishop say.

Maybe the Bee Theres should all coordinate their outfits on Tuesday night. No, that would be a mockery, and all they really wanted to do was show Sister Rhoda she wasn't with it enough to teach Beehives.

"All in favor?"

Carlie raised her hand.

Dale Delancy was sitting on the front row with the other deacons, waiting to pass the sacrament. Maybe she should ask him that very day to teach her the fine art of burping, just so she'd be prepared. Just in case.

"Any opposed?"

Carlie raised her hand. What was she going to wear on Tuesday night? What was the best way to wear the hideous fur thing Sister Durfee had given her?

She didn't realize she had done anything wrong until Bart whispered in a shocked voice, "You voted *against*."

Carlie realized that the whole congregation was quiet. From the pulpit the bishop stared straight at her. Heads turned her way.

Sister Jackson looked back at her.

Bart nudged her. "You voted *against!*" he repeated.

She saw Becca's face turned her way, and Sunshine's and Marybeth's and Elena's. They looked puzzled. This hadn't been part of the plan.

She'd been so lost in her own thoughts that she had publicly and plainly *opposed* the sustaining of Sister Jackson!

Had anybody in the whole history of the church opposed a sustaining vote?

Thank goodness her father wasn't there to see it.

She half rose out of her seat, wanting to confess that she hadn't meant to do it, that it was a mistake.

But the bishop was saying, "I'll take this up later with those who are opposed." Smoothly he went into announcing the rest of the service.

Carlie sat there numbly and worried. The other Bee Theres would probably understand that she had accidentally voted against. But what about the rest of the congregation?

And what about Sister Jackson? Would she know now that her class wanted to get rid of her?

# CHAPTER
# 9

Carlie hardly dared go to Beehive class. What would Sister Jackson say to her? With her own eyes she had seen Carlie's hand raised in a vote against her. Wouldn't she think it was deliberate?

The other Bee Theres surrounded Carlie as soon as sacrament meeting was over. Sunshine and Marybeth giggled as they took hold of an arm on either side.

"Wow," Becca breathed close to her ear. "I wouldn't have the courage to actually come right out and vote against anybody."

Even her friends thought she had deliberately voted against Sister Jackson. "I didn't mean to," Carlie whispered.

She felt as if everybody in the congregation was looking at her as they came out of the chapel into the foyer. Weren't they whispering behind their hands? What were they saying?

A flock of little kids passed, on their way to Primary. "She voted *against!*" one of the girls whispered. The whole flock paused a moment and gazed at Carlie with something like admiration.

What had she started? Would all those little Primary kids follow her example and grow up voting against the sustaining of their teachers? Would they go on to rebel against all authority figures?

Carlie groaned softly.

"Come on," Sunshine said. "Let's go to class. If Sister Jackson makes any remarks to you about voting against her, we'll all back you up. We'll just come right out and say she shouldn't be our teacher."

"I didn't mean to vote against," Carlie said softly, but nobody listened.

Maybe she wouldn't even go to class. She wasn't ready for a confrontation with Sister Jackson. Project Gross-Out had seemed far enough in the future that it was fun to think about, but this was different. This was NOW. Carlie wasn't ready right NOW, right this minute, to say to Sister Jackson's face that she didn't want her as a teacher.

"Come on," Sunshine urged, pulling at Carlie's arm. Marybeth pulled at the other, and together they towed her up the stairs to their classroom. Becca and Elena followed close behind.

At least the Bee Theres really were sticking together.

But it was one thing to be one of the supporting Bees and quite another to be the one out in front who was likely to get hashed. Would the bishop call her into his office? What would he say to her? What would she say to him?

Sister Jackson was already in the classroom when Carlie and the other girls got there. She stood at the chalkboard, writing, but she turned briefly to smile at them as they came in.

From the visual aids around the room, it was obvious that today's lesson was about keeping a journal. Sister Jackson had sketched a book on the chalkboard with the words "My Journal" printed across it. On the desk in the front of the room stood a book entitled *Women's Diaries of the Westward Journey*. Alongside it was a yellow notebook with "Journal of Rhoda Roderick" scrawled across the front in childish handwriting.

It took Carlie a moment to realize that Rhoda Roderick was indeed Sister Jackson. Roderick must have been her maiden name. For the first time Carlie wondered about Sister Jackson's husband. Other than thinking she must have tons of grandchildren, the Bee Theres hadn't even considered what kind of a family Sister Jackson had. Was her husband even alive?

Where were her children and all those grandchildren they'd decided she had?

Carlie slunk into the room and took a seat on the second row of chairs. Sunshine and Marybeth sat beside her, and Becca and Elena sat in front as if to hide her.

Sister Jackson finished what she was writing on the chalkboard and turned around. Her eyes lingered for a split second on each face in front of her, then returned to Carlie. Then they looked away, only to return once more.

"Carlie," she said, "are you all right? Your face is very flushed. Do you have a fever?"

Carlie shook her head. "No," she squeaked.

"Are you sure?" Sister Jackson came over and leaned between Becca and Elena to lay a cool palm against Carlie's forehead. Her face looked very concerned.

"Is it because of what happened in the meeting?" she asked.

Carlie nodded.

Sister Jackson laughed. "Oh, Carlie, don't worry about that. A lot of us have become mesmerized during the reading of a long list of sustainings. Once I even voted against the President of the Church right in the Tabernacle in Salt Lake City."

Becca gasped. "How come you did that?"

Sister Jackson laughed again. "Well, I was just a little girl, eight years old. I'd recently been baptized and my parents took me to general conference as a special treat. But right away I got squirmy because we'd come early to get a seat and the benches were very hard." She paused, and her eyes looked as if she were remembering.

"So what happened?" Carlie asked.

"Same thing as happened to you," Sister Jackson said. "I was admiring my new birthday ring as they read the list of General Authorities to be sustained, and I just raised my hand every time it seemed as if the man reading asked a question. I was thinking that everybody behind me could admire my new ring when I held my hand up. I realized I'd voted against the President when there was a sudden silence and everybody turned to look at me. That whole sea of faces in the Tabernacle turned toward me. All those dignified men on the stand looked down at me. Or at least I thought they did."

"So what did they do?" This time it was Sunshine who spoke.

"Nothing. I yanked my hand down and buried it in my lap. There were some chuckles around me, but everybody knew I'd just made a mistake. Just as everybody here knew you did."

Carlie laughed in relief, and the other girls

laughed too. Carlie could feel the atmosphere in the room change.

Sister Jackson smiled. "It's all right, Carlie."

She *understood*. She had once been young and foolish too.

She sympathized. She *forgave*.

Suddenly Carlie loved Sister Jackson. So what if she was perfect? Weren't they all supposed to be trying to reach a state of perfection? So what if she liked service projects? Sister Durfee wasn't all that bad.

Oh, Sister Jackson, Carlie wanted to say. You're wonderful! I'll do anything you tell me to do.

It wouldn't be hard to talk the other girls into trashing Project Gross-Out, now that they'd all seen that Sister Jackson was human after all.

But before Carlie could say anything, Sister Jackson said, "We've neglected to say the opening prayer. Becca, as class president, will you please assign someone to say it?"

Without getting up, Becca pointed to Marybeth.

Carlie almost wished she had been asked to say the prayer. She could have let Sister Jackson know in the prayer how much she appreciated her.

Marybeth got to her feet and bowed her head, but Sister Jackson held up a hand. "Wait. Let's do this properly. Becca, will you please vocalize your request?"

Becca looked bewildered. "Do what?"

"Say it. *Ask* Marybeth to please say the prayer. It's not proper just to point." Sister Jackson waited. "Do it, Becca. And please stand up this time."

Becca's bewilderment turned to a smirk. She stood up. Turning toward Marybeth, she bowed slightly and said, "Sister Marybeth, we would be ever so grateful if you would do us the honor of vocalizing the opening prayer for us."

"Becca." Sister Jackson's voice was soft but stern. "This is not the place for sarcasm. Now, do it again, this time properly."

Didn't she know Becca wasn't the one to push? Carlie held her breath, wondering whether Becca would let Sister Jackson have it, or if she'd just simply stomp out of the room. Carlie didn't see that there was a third alternative.

Becca locked gazes with Sister Jackson. What was she going to do? What had happened to the nice, warm feeling that had filled the classroom just seconds before?

Becca sucked in a deep breath. Then in a carefully controlled voice she said, "Marybeth, would you give the opening prayer, please?"

She sat down, and Carlie could see her chest fall as she let the rest of that big breath out slowly, like a slow leak of air from a tire.

Marybeth mumbled a short, fast prayer and plopped back on her chair.

"Say it again, please," Sister Jackson said as she finished. "I couldn't understand a word of it."

Marybeth stood up, closing her eyes and folding her arms across her chest like a Primary kid. She didn't say anything.

"Let it come from your heart," Sister Jackson prompted. "Don't just say the same words you've heard everybody else use."

Marybeth began mumbling again.

"Please enunciate clearly," Sister Jackson said. "You're the voice for all of us. We want to hear what you say."

Like Becca, Marybeth took a deep breath, then offered a short but clearly enunciated prayer.

"Well," Sister Jackson said when Marybeth sat down. "I can see we'd better put off this lesson about journal keeping until next week. Right now I want you to review all you learned about prayer in Primary."

As Sister Jackson turned to scrub the drawing of the journal off the chalkboard, Becca pulled a pen from her purse and wrote something across her hand. She held it up so all of the girls could see.

It said "Get rid of Rhoda!"

Quickly she licked a finger on the other hand and

erased it, just as Sister Jackson turned around again, but not before all of the girls nodded, including Carlie.

The next day at school Carlie was nervous. The bishop hadn't called her into his office after all. Did that mean he wasn't going to talk to her about voting against sustaining Sister Jackson? She almost wished he would so she could tell him how unsuitable Sister Jackson was as a Beehive teacher.

It would be nice if Gregory Okinaga and the rest of the sixth graders could know what was going on in her life. Certainly then they wouldn't think of her any longer as Miss Most Wholesome.

But would he like her any better if he knew she was really Miss Foot-in-the-Mouth, or rather Miss Hand-in-the-Air-When-It-Shouldn't-Be?

Life was hard, Carlie decided. Rather than learning about the ancient Persian Empire and how to set up an equation, why weren't they in school to study how to live life without problems? Why didn't somebody teach THAT?

The school day didn't go too badly. All of the sixth graders were looking forward to graduation, and the list of "Mosts" was almost forgotten. However, Kurt Lewis whispered to Carlie that her halo needed a little polishing that day, but that was probably because she had worn her most ratty jeans and a faded, oversized shirt. Her mother had objected to her wearing those things to school. If her mother had her way, Carlie would be back in those frilly things that had made her Most Wholesome in the first place.

Sunshine left just before school was over because she had an appointment with an orthodontist to get braces put on her teeth, so Carlie had no one to walk home with that day. Except Dale Delancy. She saw him look her way when Sunshine left and knew he would accompany her if she wanted him to.

Carlie considered walking with him. After all, Project Gross-Out was going to take place the very next night, and she could ask him for a lesson or two on Beginning Burping, just in case it failed and they had to be gross at the Couth Banquet.

But she decided she would rather walk alone than with Dale.

Mr. Most Friendly Dale. Mr. Buzzy, Buzzy Beehives Dale!

She stayed to ask Mr. Becker a question about math after class was dismissed, just long enough for Dale to leave. Then, jamming her homework into her bookbag and grabbing her purse, she started home.

Gregory Okinaga was sitting on the brick wall that surrounded the school yard. Sitting where she'd have to pass within two feet of him. His bicycle leaned against the wall near him.

Should she turn around and run? Or should she speak to him? What could she say?

She had to decide in a hurry, because she was almost there in front of him.

In desperation she decided to dig inside her purse, as if she were looking for something. That way she could look preoccupied and walk right by, unless something totally fascinating to say popped into her brain. Maybe she could ask if he was still riding his bike to school. But that would be stupid, because the bicycle sat right there. It was obvious he had ridden it. It hadn't got there by itself.

Her purse was small and crowded, and as she rummaged in it, the catnip mouse fell out. That miserable catnip mouse that had already caused her enough problems already.

So should she lean over and snatch it from the sidewalk, or should she just pretend she hadn't noticed it fall out and leave it there?

Before she could decide, Gregory jumped down from the wall and picked it up. He handed it to her without a word.

"Thanks," she mumbled. Then, thinking of Sister Jackson's instructions to "enunciate clearly," she said,

"Thank you." Now *that* was fascinating conversation, all right.

Gregory watched her stuff the mouse back inside her purse.

"Carlie," he said. "I don't mean to be rude, but do you mind if I ask you a very personal question?"

# CHAPTER 10

Carlie could feel her face burn as if there were red hot coals in the center of each cheek.

What very personal question could Gregory possibly have in mind? Was he going to ask her for a date? How could she explain to him that she couldn't date until she was sixteen?

"Carlie?" Gregory said, suddenly looking concerned when she didn't answer. She had the crazy feeling that if she didn't say something, he might reach out and press his palm against her forehead the same way Sister Jackson had done the day before.

Not trusting herself to speak, Carlie nodded, meaning yes, he could ask her the very personal question.

"Well." Now Gregory seemed reluctant to speak. He looked at the catnip mouse he still held in his hand. "Carlie, it's just this . . . well, I mean . . . " Now *his* face was getting red.

He took a deep breath, then blurted, "Carlie, does this mouse mean anything to you in a religious way?"

"Religious way?" Carlie repeated, bewildered.

"*You* know." He looked as if he wished he hadn't started this. "Like a rosary or something you always carry with you."

"This *mouse*?" Carlie could hardly believe what she was hearing.

"Well, I mean you always have it in your purse or in your pocket." He spoke rapidly. "And sometimes you chant the books of the Bible when you're doing something with it—you know, like that day you were swinging it around your head and saying 'Genesis, Exodus, Leviticus, Numbers, Deuteronomy.' So I just wondered—you know." He was fumbling for words. Gregory Okinaga, Mr. Cool himself, was fumbling for words.

Carlie wanted to laugh, but he seemed very serious.

"No," she said. "The mouse has nothing to do with anything religious."

Gregory looked relieved. "Well, one of the kids told me that you belong to this really weird religion."

"Weird?" Carlie interrupted. "What's so weird about it?"

Now Gregory looked embarrassed. He looked

away from Carlie to the San Gabriel mountains, which soared sky-tall behind them.

"I don't know," he said. "But after that person said it was weird, I started thinking she might be right if you worshipped mice or something."

Now Carlie did laugh. She wondered who was sabotaging her by saying such things, but that didn't keep her from laughing so hard she had to lean against the brick wall. Pretty soon Gregory was grinning, and then he was laughing too.

"Gregory," Carlie said as soon as she could speak. She liked saying his name. "Gregory, that mouse used to belong to Sister Durfee's cat. *Mrs.* Durfee's cat," she corrected, realizing he might think it was weird if she said "Sister." "His name is Deuteronomy."

Gregory's face brightened. "Oh, just like the old cat in that show *Cats*."

That's just what Sister Durfee had said. "Have you seen that show?" Carlie asked.

Gregory nodded. "My parents took me to it for my birthday when it was in Los Angeles. I was just a little kid, but I loved it."

"I wish I could see it," Carlie said. "I love cats."

"Me too. The show was great. Look, I'll tell you all about it while I walk you home." Gregory handed her the catnip mouse. "But first you tell me how come you're always carrying this thing with you."

That's one thing she couldn't tell him. How could she explain that she had thought it might come in handy in the project to get rid of Rhoda? But she *could* tell him about Sister Durfee and how Deuteronomy came to be lost. After all, he was the one who had given her the clue that helped her find him.

"Well, this is the way it was." She began telling him about how Sister Durfee had given her the mouse to help her find the cat.

As she spoke, she thought ahead. Was her mother going to regard walking home with a boy as a date? No, surely not. Dale Delancy had walked home with her once and had invited himself right inside for milk and cookies, and her mother hadn't objected. But Dale was a neighbor and also a Mormon. This was Gregory Okinaga, an unknown factor in the equation of Carlie's life.

She really couldn't believe that Gregory Okinaga was actually walking home with *her*. Gregory Okinaga! The other Bee Theres were going to die when she told them.

Carlie's mother didn't exactly object when the two of them arrived, but her eyes were full of questions as Carlie introduced Gregory.

It was Bart's mouth that was full of questions.

102

"Aren't you the guy who won the soccer game with Tobler School?" he asked. "Aren't you the guy who won the sixth grade Math-athon? Aren't you the guy who—"

"Bart," Carlie interrupted, "isn't there something on TV that you wanted to watch?"

"No," Bart said shortly. He hadn't taken his eyes off Gregory. "I'd rather stay here and see Gregory."

Gregory laughed. "That's okay, Bart. But how come you know so much about me?"

"Carlie talks about you all the time," Bart said. "She's got your picture up in her room."

Carlie felt her face fry again. "It's just a picture of all of us who were in the Math-athon," she said. "All of us are in the picture—you know, Kurt and Chandra and Dale and me and you and Jason." How could she shut Bart up? "Bart," she said, "were there any phone messages for me today?"

"The bishop wants you to call him," Bart said, still not taking his snaky little eyes off Gregory.

Frantically Carlie realized he wasn't through talking. Her mother must have realized it too. She walked toward Bart.

"All those girls," Bart said before anybody could stop him, "Carlie and all her friends, they sit up there in her room and look at your picture and squeal, and they drew a big red heart around your face."

103

Carlie's mother had reached Bart now. She clamped her fingers around his neck and towed him toward the kitchen. "Bart," she said, "I need you to help me make chicken teriyaki for dinner."

"I don't know how." Bart twisted around to look back at Gregory. "Are you staying for dinner, Gregory? We're having chicken teriyaki. We don't have that very often. We usually have pizza or spaghetti."

"Wish I could," Gregory said. "But I gotta go." He looked at Carlie, then away. "I gotta go."

She didn't say anything as he hurried down the porch steps, picked up his bike, threw a leg over it, and rode off as fast as he could pedal.

Carlie just stood there and watched him go. Her life was over, ruined, in ashes. How could she ever face Gregory again? How could she ever even go to school again?

"Bart," she bellowed.

Her mother came through the door from the kitchen. "I've got him busy measuring ingredients," she said. "I'm sorry he ran off the mouth so much, but don't be too hard on him, Carlie. He's just a lonely little kid, and he picks up all these things and doesn't know he shouldn't blab them all."

"Oh, Mom," Carlie wailed. "I want to strangle him."

"I know," her mother soothed, "but try to understand his problems too."

Her mother certainly didn't understand Carlie's. Oh, if only Pamela were around. Carlie could talk to her and she would sympathize and understand how awful it was to have a little brother like Bart. She'd take Carlie to the Golden Arches and they'd sit and talk until Carlie felt better. She needed a big sister so much.

But Pamela was gone, and there was for sure no possibility that Sister Rhoda Jackson would understand a single word of what Carlie needed to say.

Groaning, Carlie started for the stairs. She hoped she wouldn't see Bart anywhere, because she'd squash him for sure if she did.

"Carlie," her mother said, "Bart was right when he said the bishop called. He wants to talk to you."

Oh no, not that too. Was he going to excommunicate her right over the phone?

"He's at work, Mom. I can't call him now." Carlie knew Bishop Tolman was a lawyer, and you couldn't just call him in the middle of the day. Carlie visualized Bishop Tolman standing in front of a judge with all the jury looking at him, and he was just at the point of telling everybody who the real criminal was, since his client was innocent, when somebody tapped him on the shoulder and said, "Some girl named Carlie wants to talk to you." No, she wasn't about to interrupt something like that and make him more upset at her than he already must be.

"Call," her mother said. "He's in his office right now. He's expecting you to call back." She picked up the telephone and handed it to Carlie. "Here, I'll dial the number."

Weakly, Carlie took the telephone. She heard it buzz once, twice. "He's gone," she started to say, but right then a secretary answered.

"May I speak to Bishop Tolman?" Carlie choked out, then realized the secretary might not know who that was, since he didn't use his bishop title in his law office.

But it didn't seem like a problem for the secretary. Right away the bishop's voice came on the line.

"Hello," he boomed.

His strong voice made Carlie nervous. "This is Carlie," she said, her voice high and unsteady. "Carlie Kuramoto? From your ward? From the Beehive class?" She almost said, "The one who voted against Sister Jackson on Sunday," but she decided he probably didn't need reminding.

"I know who you are, Carlie," Bishop Tolman said. "I'm glad you called. I'm sorry I didn't get back to you on Sunday, but there were a lot of people waiting to see me."

"That's okay." Her legs felt weak, and she sat down in a chair near the phone.

"Carlie," the Bishop said, "I couldn't help but notice that you raised your hand in sacrament meeting when I asked if anyone was opposed to sustaining Sister Jackson as Beehive teacher."

"It was a mistake," Carlie whispered.

"I thought it might have been," the bishop said, "but I wanted to check it out. I want you to know, Carlie, that you have the right any time to vote against sustaining somebody if you don't think they're suitable for the job. Do you like Sister Jackson?"

What could she say? She couldn't lie, not to the bishop.

"We liked Pamela," she said softly.

"I know. Sister Sterling did a wonderful job of pulling you girls together as a class. But you know that she's going to be gone for several months."

"Couldn't we have her again when she gets back?"

"Perhaps. But she won't even be back until your first Beehive year is over."

Carlie hadn't thought of that.

"Sister Jackson has a lot to offer to your class too," Bishop Tolman continued.

"I guess so," Carlie said.

"Why don't we leave it this way?" the bishop said. "You give Sister Jackson a chance for a month, and if you're still unhappy with her, we'll see who else we can find to be your teacher. Okay?"

She hadn't come right out and said they were unhappy with Sister Jackson. It seemed to Carlie that the bishop thought her vote against her had been real. Maybe he was right. Maybe she had been so filled with bad thoughts about Sister Jackson that her hand had just automatically shot up when he asked for any opposed to manifest it.

No, she hadn't been thinking about Sister Jackson at that particular moment when she'd raised her hand at the wrong time. She'd been thinking about the fine art of burping.

"Okay," she said to the bishop, trying to remember what the question had been. Something about giving Sister Jackson a chance.

But after she'd said goodbye and hung up the phone, she wondered if it was fair to say they would give Sister Jackson a chance, when Project Gross-Out was coming up the very next night. She didn't see how she could stop that now. Once it got started, once *she* had started it, the whole thing just kept growing bigger and bigger, and she didn't think the other girls would call it off now, even if she asked them to. And she wasn't sure she wanted to, not after what had happened in class on Sunday.

No, it couldn't be turned off, any more than the

flow of words from Bart's mouth could be turned off once he had started to tell everything he knew about a subject.

"Oh, Gregory," she whispered under her breath.

For a few perfect, shining moments that day, life had seemed so wonderful.

# CHAPTER
# 11

All day Tuesday Carlie tried to avoid seeing Gregory at school. Since they were in different rooms, it wasn't too hard. She didn't even see him during the lunch period, which made her think he might be avoiding her, too.

And why wouldn't he? He probably never wanted to see her again after all those things Bart said. All those embarrassing things about how she and the other girls sighed over his picture.

That Bart! What could she do about him? She hadn't been that obnoxious when she was his age.

Or had she? She remembered when Ellen was alive and some boy named Miles had walked home with her after school. Carlie recalled that she had lurked at the front window, peeking out at them as they stood on the porch. When Miles looked her way, she had crossed her eyes, stuck out her tongue, put her thumbs in her ears, and waggled her fingers.

Miles, who had already looked embarrassed about merely standing on the same porch as Ellen, almost went into a coma when he glanced over and saw Carlie. He didn't seem to know what to do with his long arms and legs, and it wasn't long before he put his big feet into motion and left.

Carlie had thought Ellen would be angry when she came inside, but she'd grabbed Carlie up, swung her around, and said, "You little monkey. I'll never have a date if you scare all the boys away before I even get to be sixteen."

She'd never had a date, but not because Carlie scared away her boyfriends. She'd died when she was only fifteen. Carlie still missed her so much. It had been wonderful to have an understanding big sister.

Thinking about her brought Carlie's thoughts to Pamela and the way she had thought of her as a big sister. But she had lost her too, and there was no way Sister Rhoda Jackson could take the place of either Ellen or Pamela.

Well, Sister Jackson would realize that soon enough. Tonight Project Gross-Out would take place.

As they walked home together after school, Sunshine asked Carlie if she had decided what she was going to wear. "We're still meeting at my place to get dressed, aren't we?" she asked.

"Yes," Carlie said. "I think what I'll do is bring a

bunch of yucky things, and we can all decide what looks worse."

Sunshine nodded. "Be sure to bring that mangy fur thing Sister Durfee gave you. And remember that my mom has lots of stuff we can add if we need it."

That was true. Sunshine's mom had tons of big jangly jewelry and ratty sandals and saggy skirts. She was like Sunshine and looked good in things that would make anyone else look like a bag lady.

Carlie thought about herself and Sunshine and the others showing up at Sister Jackson's house all decked out in grody stuff. She thought about the way Sister Jackson hadn't blamed her when she had made a big goof of herself the day before.

"Sunshine," she said, "do you really think we're doing the right thing? I mean about Sister Jackson?"

Sunshine shifted her book bag from one shoulder to the other. "Absotively. Look, Carlie, this is the kind way to do it. Let her realize herself that she's not right as a Beehive teacher. Then she can just resign. She'll be much happier teaching 'How To Be Perfect in Three Easy Steps' in Relief Society." Sunshine turned to grin at Carlie. "Besides, it's too late to stop Project Gross-Out now."

Carlie nodded, remembering that she had thought the same thing. Trying to stop Project Gross-Out now would be like attempting to hold back a major mud-slide.

Bart was unhappy when Carlie got home.

"Those kids," he said to Carlie, "are calling me Barf again." He had probably been watching for her, because he met her at the door.

"What kids?" Why was he bothering her? She had enough of her own problems to think about.

"Those kids at my preschool. Jason and Hillary and Brent and Jennifer and—"

"What does Mom say about it?" She interrupted him before he could recite the name of every kid at the school. It sounded as if they all made fun of him.

Bart scraped a toe across the carpet. "She said to ig . . . ig . . . ig-something."

"Ignore?" Carlie asked. "Did she say to ignore them?"

Bart nodded.

"Sounds like good advice to me. Just ignore them." Carlie started up the stairs to her room. Ellen would have probably sat down with him and let him talk about it for a while. Carlie felt sorry that he had never even known his big sister.

"I can't," Bart said. "I don't know how."

"Ask Mom." Carlie hurried up a few more stairs, wishing Bart would cool it. She had to get her stuff for tonight gathered together.

113

Bart was following her. "She's busy on her computer. She said later."

"So she'll get around to it." Carlie was grateful when Bart stopped at the head of the stairs. Before she went inside her room, she leaned over the stairwell and yelled, "Mom, I'm home! Tonight's the night I'm having dinner at Sister Rhoda Jackson's house."

"I remember," her mother yelled back from the dining room, where her computer was. "Wear something nice. And do your homework first."

"Okay," Carlie yelled. She went inside her room and closed the door. Just before it shut, she glimpsed Bart sitting on the top step. Well, so what? He didn't deserve to be listened to, not after what he'd said to Gregory.

She looked around the room, thinking about what she could take over to Sunshine's house to dress in for the dinner. The fur thing, yes. But what else? What would make Sister Rhoda Jackson gasp with disgust?

On a nail above her desk hung a small plastic skull on a long leather thong, something she had won last Halloween at a party. She'd take that. Her orange high tops with the yellow polka dots. Some fake fingernails, long as a kitchen knife and painted purple. Shiny Spandex bicycle pants, hot pink with neon green stripes down the side.

She shoved all the things she selected into a brown grocery bag, then sat down to do her homework.

Bart still sat on the top step when she went downstairs later, dressed in her dark blue dress with the big splashy flowers. He leaned against the stair railing, fast asleep, his hair sticking up in untidy spikes.

Okay, so maybe he was just a lonely little kid like her mother was always saying. So maybe she'd have time later to listen to him.

She hurried past, clutching the brown bag with her gross-out stuff inside.

She stopped by the dining room table where her mother was still working. The TV was on, and a newscaster was rattling off something about a minor earthquake in the mid-part of the state.

"Just stopped by to see if I look all right." Carlie twirled in front of her mother, glad that she'd put on nylon tights and her patent leather pumps with the short heels.

Her mother leaned back in her chair. "You look wonderful, honey. Sister Jackson will be proud of you. She's looking forward to showing off her class at the Couth Youth Banquet, you know."

Carlie tried not to hear that. "Okay, Mom," she said. "I'll be over at Sunshine's. Her mother is going to drive us to Sister Jackson's and she'll bring us home."

"That's fine. Have a pleasant evening," her mother said. "I'm sure you will. Sister Jackson has a lovely home."

Carlie felt a little prickly about letting her mother think this was going to be such a nice evening. But it was all in a good cause, wasn't it? What Sunshine had said was true, that Sister Rhoda would be happier in a job more suited to her abilities.

Just as Carlie turned to go, her mother said, "What have you got in the sack?"

Carlie clutched the grocery bag closer. "Just some stuff I'm taking over to Sunshine's," she said. That was no lie. " 'Bye, Mom."

The other girls were already at Sunshine's house and almost dressed when Carlie got there.

"Hurry up, Carlie," Becca said. "I want to take a picture of all of us before we go."

Elena paraded in front of Carlie. "How do you like this?" she asked.

Her black hair was spiked. She wore a Bart Simpson T-shirt that said "Super Underachiever" on it, and a short skirt that looked as if it was made out of a heavy black plastic garbage bag, which it probably was. Elena and Sunshine were very talented at sewing.

But the best thing of all was her safety-pin earrings. She and Sunshine were the only ones in the class who had pierced ears, and now Carlie saw that Sunshine, too, had slipped large safety pins through the holes in her earlobes. She wore her jeans with the ragged knees. On top she wore a faded tie-dyed T-shirt. She had pulled one side of it through a large buckle so that it kind of rode up on her hip. Over the T-shirt she had put on a patchwork vest. On her feet were her familiar combat boots.

Marybeth wore something gauzy and bright-colored with an uneven hemline. Carlie knew it had come from Sunshine's mother's closet. With it she wore pump-up Reeboks.

Becca looked like a perfect nerd, with her hair slicked back, little round eyeglasses with a piece of white tape holding them from sliding down her nose, a plaid flannel shirt, and a pair of shapeless overalls. She stood for inspection with her chest caved in, head thrust forward, and feet, clad in white and blue wing-tip men's shoes, pointing outward.

Carlie dumped the contents of the paper bag onto Sunshine's bed and said, "Tell me what I should wear."

The other girls stirred through her stuff.

"All of it," Elena declared as Carlie started to shuck off her "nice" clothes.

"I've got just the top for you," Sunshine said, riffling through a pile of clothes on the floor. She held up a white blouse with a lacy frill down the front and lace around the cuffs of the long sleeves. "Wear this over your bicycle pants. You'll be perfect with that skull necklace hanging against the ruffles. Very wholesome."

The other girls laughed as Carlie put on the frill-loaded blouse with the Spandex pants. She shoved her feet into the orange high-tops, leaving the shoes unlaced.

Becca hung the skull around Carlie's neck, and Sunshine held up the fur thing to see how it would look best—or worst.

"We don't want to cover up those frills," she said. "How about wearing it on your head, like a turban?"

She wrapped it around Carlie's head with the two little animal faces dangling over her eyes.

"Perfect," the other girls declared.

"Oh, Carlie, it's really gross," Marybeth said.

Sunshine laughed. "Sister Jackson will positively barf."

"Speaking of such gross things," Carlie said, "did anybody learn to burp in case we need to continue this at the Couth Banquet?"

In answer, Becca took in a big gulp of air and then made a sound that would have done justice to Kurt or Dale or any of the other disgusting boys.

"Like Boy Scouts, we're prepared," she said.

"Put on your fake fingernails and let's go," Sunshine said. "I'll tell my mom we're ready."

Carlie uncapped the little bottle of glue that came with the nails. "How are you going to explain to your mom the way we're dressed?" she asked.

Carlie shrugged. "No problem. You know my mom lets me do my own thing. I just told her we're going to a dinner at Sister Jackson's. I didn't say what kind of dinner. She won't ask."

Sometimes Carlie wished her parents were as casual as Sunshine's mom was.

Sunshine was right. Her mom didn't ask about the dinner. She merely dropped off her carload of oddly dressed girls, waved, said "Have a good time," and drove away.

The five girls stood a little uncertainly in front of Sister Jackson's house. It was just through the block from Sister Durfee's house and wasn't much bigger. But there was no peeling paint on Sister Jackson's house, nor were there any weeds in the yard. Everything was perfect, like Sister Jackson.

"What are we waiting for?" Becca said. She climbed the porch steps and rang the doorbell.

Light glowed softly through the tall windows beside the door. The windows shone as if they had just been washed.

"Act cool," Sunshine whispered. "Remember, this is the way we *always* dress for parties."

The door opened suddenly and Sister Jackson stood in front of them, smiling a welcome that didn't waver as she looked them over.

"Come in," she said. "I'm so glad you're all here."

She stepped aside and they all went in. Right away Carlie's heart sank. Sister Jackson's living room looked elegant, with the sheen on the dark furniture reflecting soft lamplight. The carpet was thick and pale green. The walls were cream-colored, and the drapes were just a shade darker than the carpet.

Through an arched doorway Carlie could see a lovely table with a centerpiece of beautiful flowers. Sister Jackson had gone all out for this dinner for her class.

And there her class stood in their ratty clothes.

Sister Jackson didn't even appear to notice. "Sit down and we'll have hors d'oeuvres," she said. "I'll tell the waiters to bring them."

"Waiters?" Carlie said, as she and the other girls sat down.

Sister Jackson smiled. "I talked some neighborhood boys into acting as waiters. You girls won't have to do anything tonight except lift your forks to your mouths."

If Sister Jackson had done a double take at their

clothing, or if she had made some comment about how gross it was, or if she had given any indication at all that she even noticed, Carlie would have felt better. But Sister Jackson just continued to smile graciously as she signaled someone in the dining room to come in.

The first someone was Gregory Okinaga, carrying a silver platter heaped high with small bits of food.

Gregory Okinaga, wearing a dark suit, white shirt, and black bow tie.

Gregory Okinaga, who didn't even blink when he saw Carlie sitting there with those stupid dead animal faces hanging in her eyes.

As for Carlie, she wished that the minor earthquake upstate would suddenly become a major one and hit Sister Jackson's living room before she had to reach out and take an hors d'oeuvre from Gregory's tray.

# CHAPTER
## 12

No earthquake hit, no lightning bolt struck, no fairy godmother arrived to change Carlie's gross clothing into a beautiful ball gown.

She slid down in the soft chair so far that her chin rested on her chest. That made it so that the little animal faces on her fur turban almost totally covered her eyes, but that was all right. Maybe Gregory wouldn't be able to tell who she was.

He kept advancing sedately into the room as if he were serving hors d'oeuvres to the Queen of England. He came to stand directly in front of Carlie, bowing slightly so he could lower his tray for her to see what was on it.

"I'm Gregory," he said. "I'll be your waiter tonight."

He gave no indication that he knew who she was. Nervously Carlie reached out to take something. Anything. She'd take whatever her hand happened to light on, even liver.

She didn't look at Gregory as she selected something that had a greenish tinge. It wasn't an oyster, was it? She'd have to eat it now that she'd had her fingers on it, but she'd barf if it was an oyster.

Gregory continued to stand there. Was she supposed to tip him or something?

"Thank you," she whispered. She sneaked a look at his face, hoping he still hadn't recognized her.

"You're welcome, Carlie," he said. He was looking directly at her. His eyes were puzzled. It seemed as if he was always puzzled these days when he looked at her.

She shoved the hors d'oeuvre into her mouth. If she was chewing, she wouldn't have to say anything else to him.

It wasn't an oyster. It was some kind of pastry with spinach in it. Or maybe broccoli. It wasn't something Carlie would ordinarily eat, but with Gregory standing there watching her, she couldn't spit it out.

She chewed awkwardly, peering at Gregory from behind the little animal heads. She could hear her jaw moving. Could Gregory hear it too?

"Would you like another one?" Gregory asked, still holding the tray practically under her nose.

She shook her head, hearing little cracking sounds

in her neck bones as she did so. She swallowed the hors d'oeuvre, listening to the sound of it going down her throat, wondering why she had never noticed before how noisy and embarrassing her body was.

With a last puzzled glance at her, Gregory went on to serve Marybeth and Sunshine.

It wasn't until then that Carlie noticed that the other waiters were Jason Creeley and Kurt Lewis. Old Most-Apt-to-Start-World-War-Three Kurt. If Gregory didn't blab this whole event around school the next day, Kurt would for sure.

Sister Jackson was going from girl to girl, smiling, speaking softly, being gracious.

Carlie wasn't quite sure where she got that word. Probably from some book she had read, because she didn't remember that it had ever passed her lips. But that's what Sister Jackson was. Gracious.

Well, so what? She still wasn't Pamela. And this evening was not about being gracious. It was about grossing out.

But how were they going to gross out with Gregory and Jason and even Kurt looking and acting so sharp?

Becca was staring at Kurt as if she had never seen him before.

As Carlie watched, she hid her bare feet under the edge of the sofa. Sunshine's face was like a flaming sunset as she picked something from Jason's tray.

When the three boys finished their rounds with the hors d'oeuvre trays, they filed back into the kitchen. With an "Excuse me for a moment," Sister Jackson followed them.

As soon as they were gone, Sunshine took the safety pins from her ears and quickly began pinning together the ragged holes in the knees of her jeans. "Why did Sister Jackson ask *them* to be waiters?" she asked frantically. "Why didn't she get those nerdy Scouts from church?"

She sounded as if she thought Sister Jackson did it just to be mean.

"She said they live nearby," Carlie said, bending over to lace up her orange high-tops. She whipped off the skull necklace and jammed it in her little purse, but there wasn't a whole lot more she could do to improve her appearance, except maybe ditch the fur turban. But where would she put it? No, better to leave it. Gregory had already seen it anyway. Twisting it around, she fixed it so the animal faces dangled down in back rather than over her eyes.

"Besides," Elena said, still on Sunshine's question, "the church guys are probably somewhere practicing for the Couth Youth Banquet too." She tried to smooth down her spiked hair, but all she succeeded in doing was make it stick out in a few more new directions.

Becca rolled her eyes. "Well, I feel sorry for whoever is trying to teach decent manners to those nerdy Scouts."

Carlie nodded. But were those nerdy Scouts any worse than they were, sitting there in Sister Jackson's lovely, perfect living room and looking like a bunch of escapees from the city dump?

She watched Elena try to pull her short garbage-bag skirt down over her knees. Becca had removed the little round eyeglasses that had been taped to her nose, and now she was twitching her overalls around, trying to give them a little shape.

"How could she do this to us?" she moaned.

Privately Carlie thought they had done it to themselves, but she didn't say anything. Besides, Sister Jackson had come back from the kitchen now and was heading right for her.

"Carlie, I'm so glad you could come," she said in that soft voice she had used as she spoke to the others. She smiled, but Carlie thought that her eyes looked a little sad.

"I understand you're giving a speech at your sixth grade graduation exercises next week," Sister Jackson went on.

Carlie nodded. "I'm speaking about finding the right path for you. I mean for each person. I mean each person should find the right path for them. I mean him. Her."

Sister Jackson smiled. "I understand. I gave the eighth grade valedictory speech in my little country school many years ago. My favorite teacher gave me a quotation to build my talk around. It was, 'Not failure but low aim is crime.' She knew I needed to think about that, and it helped me to go for what I really wanted."

Sister Jackson stood up quickly without a single knee creak or helping hand. She was a whole lot more agile than Grandma Kuramoto. But that was part of her whole perfection image.

Was perfection what she had decided to go for?

Carlie didn't have much time to think about what she had said because Sister Jackson was announcing dinner.

"You've all done very well on the appetizer course," she said. "Now we'll go on to the main event. Come into the dining room and look for a place card with your name on it."

All of the girls stood and walked toward the dining room. Nobody looked much better despite their efforts to improve their appearance. Sunshine's torn jeans looked worse with the big safety pins holding them together. Elena's spiked hair had begun to droop and look tired.

Carlie slunk along with the others, searching for her name on a place card on the table. She found she was to sit between Elena and Sister Jackson.

How could she eat, seated next to Sister Jackson and served by Gregory and the other guys? And what was she supposed to do with all of the silverware? It seemed as if there were extras of everything, including a third fork that lay at the top of her place mat. She wondered if it was a mistake, but there was one at every place.

After the girls were all seated, Sister Jackson called to the boys. They came in, and Gregory walked right over to Carlie. Without a word he pulled her flower-folded napkin from where it grew in her empty water glass, snapped it smartly open, and laid it across her lap. He went on to do the same thing for the other girls and Sister Jackson.

Kurt poured water into all the glasses, and Jason served the first course.

Carlie wasn't sure what it was. It was on a little plate, and it looked like a small, green pineapple. Gregory came by and left a tiny dish full of melted butter.

"As you may know," Sister Jackson said, "the planners of the Couth Youth Banquet always serve foods that are a challenge to eat. I have no idea what the menu will be this year, but I thought I'd acquaint you with some possibilities." Reaching out to her green thing, she pulled off a bottom leaf. "These are artichokes," she said, "and this is how you eat them." Dipping the leaf into the melted butter, she put it between her teeth, clamped down, and pulled, apparently keeping part of it in her mouth. She then put the used leaf back on the plate at the side of the artichoke.

Each girl followed her example. Carlie thought the part of the artichoke leaf that she ate didn't taste too bad, but was it worth the effort? Mostly she liked the melted butter, but you could get the same benefit from buttered popcorn, which was a whole lot easier to eat.

There was total silence as they ate their artichokes, except for an occasional slurp when someone clamped down too hard before she pulled out a leaf. Carlie got along fine until she was almost finished. Then somehow a hunk of leaf got jammed between her upper front teeth. She tried to work it out with her tongue, but it wouldn't budge. She was glad Gregory had gone back to the kitchen.

"Now, that wasn't too bad, was it?" Sister Jackson asked when everyone was finished and she signaled the guys to take the little plates away. "We're ready for the salad now."

The guys came back, carrying a green salad for each person. Carlie knew the small outer fork was the

correct one to use for that, so the salad was no challenge except she worried about that artichoke piece
wedged in her front teeth. She kept her head down
so Gregory wouldn't see it.

"The main course," Sister Jackson said as the guys
brought in plates loaded with food, "is half a guinea
hen, green peas, and rice pilaf." Then, as the guys set
a plate in front of each girl, she said, "I've been wondering what you think about the new movie on at the
Hastings Theater. The one about mind control. Do
you think something like that could really happen?"

"Yeah, man, I sure hope so," Kurt said, putting a
plate at Becca's place. "I'm going to be one of the
controllers."

Gregory nudged him, probably reminding him
that waiters didn't take part in the conversation. Actually, Carlie had been surprised that Kurt hadn't said
something before about the girls' grody clothes or
about the artichokes or something. It wasn't like Kurt
to behave himself.

"I disagree," Marybeth said. "I think we're too
smart for that ever to happen."

"But the way it was in the movie," Sunshine said,
"you couldn't help it no matter how smart you were."

Sister Jackson was pretty smart herself, to get a
conversation going about something they were all in-

terested in. Carlie was surprised that she had even seen the movie, which was aimed at teenagers.

Carlie wanted to say something about the movie, but she couldn't with that gross thing sticking in her teeth. She continued to sit with her head ducked, but that made her fur turban slip further and further down over her forehead. She was having trouble with the rice pilaf, too, which wouldn't stay on her fork. With each bite she took, she left a trail of kernels all across her lap.

She wasn't the only one having trouble. Becca tried to stab her half of a bird with her fork so she could cut off some meat with her knife, but she succeeded only in scooting the whole thing onto the floor. She blushed as she snatched it up and put it back on her plate.

But Kurt smoothly whisked the whole plate away and brought Becca another one. Carlie was surprised that he didn't comment on it.

Marybeth launched a forkful of peas all over the table when she tried to eat and defend her position about the movie at the same time.

But the worst moment came when the guys brought in the dessert, a flat piece of chocolate cake with a blood-red raspberry sauce over it.

This was too much for Kurt. His self-control, stretched to the max, snapped.

"It's called Dracula's Delight," he hissed as he placed a dessert in front of each girl. "Check your necks for punctures. Watch out for low-flying bats."

Carlie couldn't help but giggle along with the other girls. Not wanting to show the artichoke hunk in her teeth, she ducked her head even further, which dislodged her fur turban entirely. It fell into the raspberry sauce, with the little dead faces staring up at her.

Kurt spotted it right away. "Road kill, road kill, look at the blood," he chortled. Snatching it, he flung it to Gregory.

Carlie wanted to disappear.

But Gregory, instead of carrying on the game, said, "Come on out to the kitchen, Carlie, and we'll clean this off."

Wordlessly, Carlie slid back her chair, stood up, and somehow followed him into the kitchen.

Gregory was at the sink, dabbing at the fur with a damp dishcloth. "I'm sorry Kurt lost it," he said. "Mrs. Jackson told us we had to behave. She's a neat lady."

Carlie just stood there, not wanting to open her mouth and reveal the thing in her teeth.

"She told us she wanted to show us some really good examples of the young people from her church." He turned to hand her the cleaned-up fur. "That's why we're here."

Carlie couldn't tell from his eyes what he thought of the "good examples." But as he looked at her, Carlie wished her fairy godmother would hurry and get around to that instant change of clothes. Forget the beautiful ball gown. She'd settle for her red-dotted outfit. The frilly one. The *wholesome* one.

So what had happened to Project Gross-Out?

# CHAPTER
# 13

The next morning Carlie was later than usual getting to school. Sunshine was already in their room, and they didn't have time to discuss anything before class started. But she passed Carlie a note that said, "Gregory was looking for you," followed by five exclamation points.

Gregory looking for her? He probably just wanted to rag on her about how awful she and the others had been the night before. He had made that remark in the kitchen about Sister Jackson being so nice, and he obviously wondered why the girls were dressed in ratty clothes for such a fancy dinner. Then later she had caught him watching her a couple of times, even after she'd finally got the piece of artichoke out of her teeth.

Well, she would just make sure he didn't find her today. She didn't need any more downers.

Avoiding him wasn't too hard, since there were lots of places to hide around the school. At noon she talked Sunshine into eating lunch behind an oleander bush on the north lawn. Gregory would never think of looking for her there.

Sunshine had things on her mind, too. "What are we going to do now that Project Gross-Out failed?" she asked as she put her lunch on the grass and sat down beside it. "Are we going to go ahead with our backup plan to get rid of Rhoda at the Couth Youth Banquet?"

Carlie thought about how nice Sister Jackson had been to all of them, and about that small, sad look on her face when she had first seen them in their scruffy clothes. She wanted to talk about it, to say maybe they should just forget about getting rid of her.

But how could they ever hope to get a suitable Beehive leader if they quit now? And how could she back down anyway? What would the other girls think?

"Yes," she said. "We'll call an emergency meeting of the Bee Theres for tonight to make our final plans." She bit down on the slice of pizza she'd brought from the cafeteria. It tasted more like cardboard than usual.

Or maybe she just didn't have much of an appetite.

Sunshine hesitated just a moment before she nodded. "Okay. I'll call Elena and Marybeth. You call Becca."

They ate the rest of their lunches in silence.

Carlie successfully avoided Gregory all day, but when she got home, Bart met her at the door saying there had been a phone call for her. Gregory! He must be trying to reach her by telephone, since he hadn't been able to find her in person.

But Bart said, "It was Sister Durfee. She wants you to come read to her for a while this afternoon."

Carlie was surprised at the way her heart sank. It was as if she actually was hoping it had been Gregory who had called.

Bart pulled at her sleeve. "Can I go too?"

"No," Carlie said. That's all she needed right now, to have not only Sister Durfee to put up with but also Bart.

"Why not?" Bart shifted to his whiny voice.

"Because."

"Because why?"

Carlie sighed. "Because *because*."

"You can't say 'because because,'" Bart said. "You have to say why because."

It was too much for Carlie. "Will you cut it out, Bart?"

Her voice must have been louder than she thought, because from the dining room her mother called, "What's going on in there?"

"He's bugging me, that's what's going on," Carlie called back.

"Carlie, be nice to him. He's lonely."

If Carlie had kept count of how many times her mother had said that, she was sure it would number in the thousands. Millions maybe.

She wanted to screech to Bart that he made her life miserable, that he was a whiny little pest, that he really was a barf like the other kids said.

But he would just go right on being a pest. Sighing, she sat down on a chair.

"Come here, Bart." She reached out for him.

He came to her without question, standing in the circle of her arms and looking straight at her. Looking at her the same way Carlie had once stood within Ellen's arms and looked at her, waiting for her to say something important.

"Bart," she said, "I can't take you with me because Sister Durfee is not used to having kids around."

"Oh." Bart nodded solemnly. "Doesn't she have any kids?"

Carlie realized she didn't know. "If she does, they've all grown up and gone away."

"Doesn't she get lonesome?" Bart looked concerned.

"Maybe," Carlie said. "But she has her cat. His name is Deuteronomy. He's big and orange and has humongous green eyes. When he purrs he sounds as if there's a little motor inside him."

Bart looked pleased. "Does he listen when you read?"

"Yes." Carlie stood up, taking her arms from around Bart. "Now I've got to see if Mom can take me over there so I can get the reading over with."

Bart still stood close to her. "Carlie?" he said.

"What?" He'd better not start whining again. She wasn't up to dealing with it, not right now with all she had to think about.

He leaned against her. "I like it when you have time to talk to me."

Memories swept over Carlie. Memories of Ellen, who had never been too busy to talk to her. She'd been such a great big sister.

Looking down at Bart, Carlie realized for the first time that *she*, Carlie, was the big sister now.

Pushing the thought away, she said, "Bart, I'll talk to you later. I have to go."

He followed her into the dining room, where their mother worked at her computer.

"Mom," Carlie said, "I have to go read to Sister Durfee. Can you drop me off? And is it okay if I have dinner at McDonald's with Sunshine and Becca and the others?"

Her mother smiled a little as she shut down her

computer. "McDonald's would go out of business if you girls decided to eat at home more often."

But she didn't say Carlie couldn't go.

Sister Stella Durfee was waiting on her front porch beside her red door when Carlie got to her house.

"Took you long enough," she said as Carlie climbed the stairs.

The day had been too much for Carlie. She was in no mood for Sister Durfee's little jabs. "Sorry," she snapped. "Maybe I should quit school so I can get here immediately whenever you want me."

As soon as she had said the words, Carlie regretted them.

Sister Durfee blinked. "Tongue like a whip," she commented. Suddenly she grinned. "I like that in a person. Come on in." She stood back so Carlie could go past her into the house.

Sister Durfee grinning? What next? Would the sky fall?

Carlie went into the cluttered living room. Deuteronomy greeted her with a throaty meow from his place on the back of the sofa. The sun shining through the prism on the windowsill made bright spots of color all around the room. The green wing chair welcomed her with its usual comfortable sag as she sat down.

Sister Durfee eased herself into her old brown

chair. "Understand it's your Couth Youth Banquet tomorrow night."

Sister Jackson must have told her. What else had she passed along? Had she entertained Sister Durfee with all the events of the night before?

"Yes," Carlie said warily.

Sister Durfee stirred through the stack of books on the little table beside her chair. She handed Carlie a thick volume. "Let's read from this today."

Carlie took the book. It was entitled *Major Disasters of the World*.

What was Sister Durfee implying? Was she making fun of her?

Carlie thrust the book back at Sister Durfee. "No," she said firmly. "Pick something else."

Sister Durfee squinted at her. "You're here to read what I want to hear."

Carlie shook her head. "I'll read from the *Ensign* or the *Reader's Digest* or the romance books, but if you want this one, you'll have to read it yourself."

"Atta girl," Sister Durfee said. "The romance it is."

Surprised, Carlie took the book Sister Durfee held out to her. That hadn't been the reaction she had expected from Sister Durfee. She wasn't quite sure what to do.

Sister Durfee was grinning again. "You never know, do you, Carlie?" she said.

What was she talking about? Books? People? What?

Maybe all of the above.

Suddenly Carlie grinned too. Settling back in the familiar chair, she opened the book and began to read. They were at a thrilling part. Megan, the heroine who worked in the sports store, had agreed to go bungee-cord jumping with rich, handsome, athletic Trevor, to make him think she shared his interests. Elwood, the tax accountant, was trying to talk some sense into her head before she broke it. Vanessa, the girl who loved Trevor, was trying to get to the bungee cords so she could cut Megan's partly in two before the jump.

The chapter ended with Megan standing with Trevor on a high bridge, ready to jump. Would she go, or wouldn't she? Had Vanessa been successful in cutting the cord?

Carlie would like to have read another chapter, but it was time to meet the other Bee Theres.

She closed the book. "I have to go," she told Sister Durfee.

"I hope I can wait until Friday," Sister Durfee said. "I don't suppose you'll be coming tomorrow, what with the banquet and all."

For a change she wasn't giving commands. "I'll come Friday," Carlie agreed.

McDonald's was close enough that she could walk there from Sister Durfee's. As she went along, she half-expected to see Gregory suddenly appear on his bike, the way he had a couple of times before.

But he didn't.

The emergency meeting of the Bee Theres at the Golden Arches didn't go well either. Everybody seemed edgy. And nobody had any great ideas about what they should wear to the banquet the following night, or what they should do when they got there.

"At this rate, we're never going to get rid of Rhoda," Marybeth said, as she dipped a french fry into a puddle of ketchup. She looked at Carlie.

The others looked at Carlie too.

They clearly expected her to come up with some fantastic idea, some solution to their problem. Well, why not? The "Getting Rid of Rhoda" project had been her idea in the first place.

What could she say? That she'd changed her mind? That she couldn't bear to see that sad look on Sister Rhoda's face again if they embarrassed her in front of all the others at the banquet?

Was it that she hated having Gregory think badly of her for not being nice to Sister Jackson?

No, of course not. "Let's do the unexpected," she said, remembering how she had floundered when Sister Durfee had done the unexpected. "Sister Jackson will be expecting us to come to the banquet looking as dumpy as we did last night. Instead, let's be couth to the max. Well, at least as far as our clothes are concerned."

The other girls thought about it. They smiled.

"We'll all be Rhoda clones," Becca said.

"Coordinated clothes," Sunshine said. "Majorly neat."

"Starched hair." Elena tossed her head so that her dangly earrings danced.

"We'll talk about service projects," Marybeth said.

"That will really throw her," Sunshine said.

"We can each do our own thing from there on in," Becca suggested. "Go with the flow. Do whatever seems right at the moment."

"Or wrong," Sunshine said, and they all laughed.

Everybody seemed satisfied with the plan. Certainly it would confuse Sister Jackson.

But Carlie still felt uneasy. Would Sister Jackson feel they were making fun of her if they all showed up dressed to perfection? Would she feel mocked? Would she tell Gregory and those other guys about it?

Carlie thought about that. Was that why she had suggested dressing up in the first place? Just to impress Gregory in case he heard about it?

Suddenly she felt like the romance heroine she

143

had just been reading about to Sister Durfee. She was Megan, trying to impress Trevor. But she was also Vanessa, sawing her own bungee cord in two, because she would definitely wipe herself out in Gregory's eyes if she hurt Sister Jackson again and he heard about it.

# CHAPTER
## 14

Carlie had trouble sleeping that night. It hadn't helped her much to realize she was the big sister now and that Bart looked up to her the way she used to look up to Ellen. She still needed someone to talk to, someone with a lot of good sense but who would still understand the dilemmas of a twelve-year-old. Big sister or not, she couldn't very well talk things over with herself.

Or could she?

She imagined two of herself facing each other. One self was small and wimpy and all hunched over with problems she couldn't solve. Her hair was ratty, and she wore torn jeans and a shirt whose sleeves were too long.

The other stood up straight and held her head high and wore glasses. That self had neat hair and wore a turquoise suit with matching shoes.

Sister Jackson! She was seeing her wise self as Sister Jackson! She must be having a nightmare.

She squeezed her eyes tightly shut and changed the scene. She thought about the Bee Theres, but that only brought Sister Jackson back into her mind.

Thinking about Gregory didn't help either, because again Sister Jackson poked right up in plain sight.

Frantically Carlie shifted gears completely. She thought about school. About math class. About history. About English exams.

Pretty soon she was asleep.

The next day it was Dale Delancy who told her Gregory had been looking for her. She was late to school again because she had overslept, and she met Dale on the stairs leading down to their classroom.

"Greg ever find you yesterday?" Dale asked. "He was looking all over for you."

"I didn't see him," Carlie said shortly. She didn't want to talk to Dale about Gregory.

Dale shrugged. "No sweat. I think he just wanted to tell you he'd see you tonight."

"Tonight?"

"Guess he's coming to the banquet. Did you invite him?"

Carlie shook her head. Very likely Sister Jackson had invited him and the other guys to come to the

146

banquet and be the waiters, since they had done such a good job at her house.

So how did that affect the Bee Theres? They had already decided to dress for success, so Gregory wouldn't be getting on her case about that. He didn't know they were doing it to confuse Sister Jackson, and he didn't have to know. All he would see was that the girls were dressed appropriately that night. And if gross things happened—well, how could a person avoid accidents? Gregory wouldn't have a clue as to what was really going on.

Carlie realized that Dale was still speaking and she hadn't heard a word of what he said.

"I'm sorry," she said. "What did you say?"

"I said, are you ready for tonight?" Dale raised his voice as if the reason she hadn't heard was because she was hard of hearing.

"Ready for what?" Carlie wasn't sure what he was talking about, even though she heard the words.

"Ready for the Couth Youth Banquet. We had a Scout dinner last night, and one of us is going to win the King of Couth crown."

"You mean you really *want* to win?"

Dale grinned. "Sure."

"Why?"

"Why not? Seems like a good thing to do. The guy who wins will get his picture in the ward newspaper and everybody will know he's not a goof-off *all* the time."

Carlie didn't know it mattered to Dale whether everybody thought he was a goof-off or not.

"So," he said, "are you ready?"

"Yes," Carlie said. "I'm ready."

She guessed she was. All she had to do was decide which one of her good dresses Sister Jackson would be most likely to pick if she were choosing.

Actually, the way it turned out, she chose the dress that matched her blue shoes, just so she'd be coordinated. It was a pretty dress, one of her favorites, so she was happy with it. It had short sleeves and a full, swingy skirt.

Her father was cooking dinner that night, so her mother had time to do her long black hair in a French braid, which was just about her favorite way to wear it when she wanted to look nice.

"This banquet is such a good idea," her mother said as she pulled the strands of Carlie's hair into place. "You young people today have so few things to really dress up for. When I was a girl we enjoyed getting spiffed up."

Carlie remembered the pictures of her mother as a young girl in the family photograph album. She had worn sleeveless A-line dresses and little white gloves, and her hair had been teased into a high, stiff tower, not all that different from Sister Jackson's.

Maybe the Bee Theres should have gone in for something like that. Sister Jackson would probably have felt right at home with those fashions.

Bart came wandering into the family room just then.

"Wow!" he said. His eyes were big.

Her mother was finished with her hair, so Carlie stood up. "Do I look all right, Bart?" She twirled around so that her skirt swished around her legs.

"Wow!" Bart repeated. "Carlie, you look mega-pretty."

Carlie's father appeared in the doorway holding a wooden spoon that he had apparently been stirring something with. "Oh my," he said. "Oh my."

Carlie figured he would launch into his "My little girl is all grown up" routine next, but he didn't because Sunshine came bursting into the room at just the right time.

"Hi, everybody," she sang out. "Carlie, Mom'll drive us to the bishop's house."

Sunshine wore a dress that actually had frills, and what's more, she looked great in it. It was a summer-green color, just right for Sunshine's long blonde hair, which was held back with a green headband.

Carlie's dad waved his spoon. "Tell your mother

to stop by on her way home and share our dinner. We'll talk about our beautiful daughters."

Sunshine smiled. "Will do. Come on, Carlie."

Suddenly Carlie wasn't at all sure she wanted to go to the banquet. She felt as if she were one big, total lie. If her outside looked like her inside felt, her parents wouldn't be gazing at her with all that pride. They would step back so they wouldn't be splattered by the slime and ooze, because that's the way she felt inside.

Messes are a whole lot easier to get into than out of, that was for sure. She wished she could push a cancel button like on her mother's computer and see the whole Rhoda project just disappear from her life.

But Sunshine was waiting.

"See you later, kiddo," Carlie said to Bart. She blew kisses to her mom and dad and hurried out the door with Sunshine.

A lot of people were already at the bishop's house when Carlie and Sunshine got there. Several of the older girls were standing together in the living room, whispering and giggling and casting glances at a bunch of guys who were clumped near some shelves that displayed athletic trophies. Both girls and guys were dressed nicely and were obviously trying their best to be couth.

Dale Delancy was there, with his wrists hanging out of his blue suit jacket, which had become too small just in the last couple of months. His hair looked freshly cut, and there were damp comb tracks in it.

He really did look as if he were out to get that King of Couth crown. He and the other Scouts were on their best behavior, although they weren't exactly at ease.

Sister Jackson was there with the other adult leaders. As usual, she was perfect in a pinkish purple suit and a darker pink blouse with pearls. Her hair glistened with hair spray, as if she had just come from the beauty salon, which she probably had.

"Carlie," she said when the girls came in. "And Sunshine. How sweet you both look."

They smiled and said, "Thank you."

Carlie felt as ill at ease as the Scouts looked.

"Those young men from my street are here tonight," Sister Jackson said. "They asked if they could come and help out."

"They *asked* to come?" Carlie wondered if she was hearing right.

"Yes," Sister Jackson said. "Gregory told me his older brother worked his way through college as a waiter in a fancy restaurant. Gregory said he was really happy to learn a useful skill."

So that was why he was there. Not to see her or even to be critical of her. He was there to practice a "useful skill."

Becca, Marybeth, and Elena arrived just then. Becca and Marybeth were in flowered dresses with lacy collars. Elena, who could whip out a new dress on her sewing machine before you could say "Let's go shop," had made a two-piece pink flowered suit and then had covered her high-heeled white pumps with some of the same material. She wore her mother's pearls.

She looked like a smaller, younger Sister Jackson. But she didn't look all that happy about it.

Neither did Sister Jackson. That sad look flitted across her face as she greeted the three girls, but all she said was, "How very nice you all look."

She was getting the message all right.

Somebody rang a little dinner bell, and Sister Blake, the Young Women president, motioned for everyone to be quiet. "As soon as the waiters put the first course on the tables, we want you all to go around and find the place card with your name on it. Remember now, you're being judged on your manners, your conversation, your clothes, and whether you remembered to RSVP on time."

There were some groans in the room, which indicated that some kids had forgotten to RSVP, which would cost them a point.

Sister Jackson smiled at her class. "You're all going

to do very well," she said, then went to look for her place card.

"Hey, you guys," Carlie whispered. "I want to say something."

"Say it after dinner," Elena said. "We're supposed to go eat now."

"That's what I want to say something about," Carlie said.

Just then Gregory came into the room carrying a large tray. On it was . . . Carlie couldn't believe her eyes. Artichokes!

She heard one of the older guys whisper, "What are those?"

"Hey," Becca said. "Sister Jackson picked one thing right. We know how to eat those. We could ace this thing tonight, if we wanted to."

They could, thanks to Sister Jackson. Thanks to her they too had some "useful skills," more than just knowing how to eat artichokes.

So why were they trying to get rid of her? What had she done that was so bad, except not be Pamela? Maybe they were ready to go on to something besides sleepovers and miniature golf, the way Carlie was ready to go on from little sister to big sister.

"Let's forget about getting rid of Rhoda," she blurted out.

To her surprise, the other girls smiled broadly.

"I was hoping you'd say that," Elena whispered back. "I don't feel right about our project anymore, but I didn't want the rest of you to think I was wimpy."

The others nodded. They all looked relieved.

Carlie realized that everyone had been waiting for somebody else to speak up. Well, she'd be the one.

"Come on," she said. "Let's win the Queen of Couth crown. Let's win it for Rhoda."

Actually it was Elena who won the crown. She got a perfect score, eating the artichoke, the chicken Kiev, the au gratin potatoes, and the green salad with cherry tomatoes without a single accident. Carlie, Sunshine, Becca, and Marybeth lost one point each for small things, like when Sunshine tried to slice her Chicken Kiev and it squirted butter onto a judge's tie.

Dale Delancy won the King of Couth crown.

When the bishop announced the winners, he commented that never before had both winners been from the youngest group of kids.

Sister Jackson beamed with pride, and the Scout leader led his Scouts in a cheer.

Then, to the surprise of Carlie and the other Beehive girls, the bishop said, "We're going to relax now and have Sister Jackson entertain us at the piano."

Carlie didn't even know she played the piano. She

expected that Sister Jackson would sit down and pound out some hymns or something, but instead she slid onto the piano bench, winked at the crowd, and, after a couple of rousing chords, launched into a crazy song about chicken lips and lizard hips. Then before everyone stopped laughing about that one, she went into one called "Shootin' with Rasputin' " and another one about midnight on the ocean.

After that she had everyone sing "Oh, the horse went around with his foot off the ground," and "There's a hole in the bottom of the sea."

Everybody clapped and yelled for more. Carlie and the other Bee Theres clapped louder than anybody else. This was their teacher. They wanted everybody to know that.

"More," everybody yelled.

But Sister Jackson said it was time to go, since there was school the next morning.

When Carlie turned to look for Sunshine, she saw Gregory Okinaga standing a few feet behind her.

"Carlie," he said over the noise of the other kids, "I've been wanting to talk to you."

He pointed toward the kitchen, and she followed him out there.

"Carlie," he said when the door swung shut and he could be heard, "you guys were really great tonight."

"Thanks," she said. Her mouth felt dry and her tongue was a lump of fur.

"I wasn't sure what was going on Tuesday night," Gregory said. "I mean, the clothes and all. But tonight you really came through."

"Thanks," Carlie said again. So was her replay button stuck on that word? "What did you want to talk to me about?"

Gregory shook his head. Looking at the floor, he followed a line in the linoleum with one toe.

"Carlie, I know you can't date or anything like that until you're sixteen. Sister Jackson told me. But could I invite you to do the dishes with me? I volunteered to take care of them. Mrs. Jackson said she'd take you home if you could stay." He said it all in one breath, as if he had it memorized.

Carlie laughed. Had a girl ever had a more romantic invitation? "I'll have to call my folks," she said. "But I'd really like to do dishes with you."

Gregory raised his head, and Carlie saw that he was blushing. Actually blushing!

"Carlie," he said. "You're so different from most girls. You're so . . . so . . . "

"Wholesome?" Carlie provided the word.

Gregory grinned. "Yeah. Wholesome."

Somehow it didn't sound like the end of the world anymore.

When Lael Littke was a Beehive girl in Mink Creek, Idaho, she loved to ride her horse and dream of someday living in a big city where she would be a writer. Now that she lives in Pasadena, California, and has written twenty-six books, she loves to remember those wonderful days when she was young. Besides books, she enjoys writing roadshows for the young people of her ward in Pasadena Stake. The widow of George Littke, she has one daughter and a houseful of cats and dogs.

## Other Books You'll Enjoy from Deseret Book and Cinnamon Tree

*The Mystery of Ruby's Ghost,* Book 2 in the Bee There Series, by Lael Littke

*Where the Creeks Meet* by Lael Littke

Lucky Ladd Series: *Lucky's Crash Landing, Lucky Breaks Loose, Lucky's Gold Mine, Lucky Fights Back, Lucky's Mud Festival, Lucky's Tricks,* and *Lucky the Detective,* by Dean Hughes

*The Williams Family Series: Under the Same Stars, As Wide as the River,* and *Facing the Enemy* by Dean Hughes

*The Other Side of the Door* and *Climbing Up the Rainbow* by Joy Hulme

*Enchantress of Crumbledown* by Donald R. Marshall

*A Lasting Peace* by Carol Lynn Pearson

*The Magic Garden* by Greg Larson

*The Lord Needed a Prophet* by Susan Arrington Madsen

*The Mormon Church: A Basic History* by Dean Hughes